MY SON DAN
by Lettie Wheeler Moore

Pacific Press Publishing Association
Mountain View, California
Omaha, Nebraska   Oshawa, Ontario

Dedicated

with love to
all my grandchildren, and to Dan, whose life, a
living miracle, is being used to glorify God,
and to all the dear ones that God has brought
me throughout the years.

Foreword

A few years ago, it was my privilege to meet Dan Collins. His exuberant spirit affected me in such a way that I have never forgotten him, although our paths seldom cross. His Christian spirit and personality make an indelible impression upon anyone he meets.

When we first met, he said nothing to me about his past experiences, but his life made such an impact on me that I wanted to know more about how he became a minister. This led to a taped interview, which eventually became a part of our General Conference Ministerial Association Tape Club. We probably have had more requests for duplicates of this remarkable story than for any other tape produced.

In my conversation with Dan, one point impressed me: He takes no delight in discussing or talking about his infamous past life. Like the apostle Paul, he relates the unsavory events of his youth only to demonstrate that a lost soul can never get beyond the reach of God.

The new-birth experience, wherein a sinful life is changed into Christ likeness, is always a miracle, but there are probably not many such changes that equal the drama of the one recorded in this book. Yet this change in Dan Collins's life did not come about without a struggle on his part. The transformation of Dan, alcoholic, transient and ne'er-do-well, to Dan, minister of the gospel of Jesus Christ and ambassador of the kingdom of grace, is so remarkable as to be considered unbelievable. But for those of us who know the mighty ability of our God to give new hearts to sinners, the story is not so surprising as it is reassuring. It strengthens our belief that the God of heaven can indeed overcome any and all obstacles.

What God did for Dan Collins, He is willing and able to do for any lost child who is discouraged and sinking because of continued failure. It is my deep conviction that the readers of this book not only have in store a rich and delightful reading experience, but will surely gain greater courage and confidence to trust God for His mighty power in changing our lives and keeping them changed.

J. R. Spangler, Associate Director, Ministerial Association
General Conference of Seventh-day Adventists

Contents

Dan and Kay Collins,
who have dedicated their lives to service.

1

Sadness and Joy

Mother Collins guided her two boys, Don and little Albert Dean, dressed in their Sunday best, toward the front door. She paused at the door and turned to her husband as he came into the room. "I see you're ready to work. I do wish you'd come to church with us."

Father Collins shook his head. "No, Mother, there's too much to do around here. I'm glad you take the boys."

Mother sighed. Then putting a hand on each boy's shoulder she urged them out the door.

There had been an ache in Mother Collins's heart for many years because her husband, although brought up a staunch Methodist in belief, neglected church attendance.

But each Sunday at church her anxieties seemed to fade away. How she loved to fellowship with like believers in God's house and to share in the blessings of worship! It gave her strength for the week to come.

Back at home after the service, Mother sang as she hurried with preparations for Sunday dinner. The boys changed into their play clothes. Then, as she put the plates on the table, she called, "Boys, it's time to get Daddy. Dinner's almost ready."

Away ran Don with little Albert Dean following as fast as his shorter legs could manage. Mother watched out the window as the children grabbed their father when he came out of the barn. Laughing and chattering as they walked, the three came to the house.

"Me go Sunny Cool," she heard little Albert Dean say as they came in. "You go Sunny Cool too, Daddy?"

"Sometime I'll go with you, Sonny," she heard her husband answer. "Someday!"

But Sundays came and went. From time to time little Albert Dean queried, "Daddy, you go Sunny Cool today?"

"One of these days," his father would reply.

One Sunday morning when Albert Dean awoke he complained, "My head hurts. I too hot." He pushed back the covers.

Mother Collins put her hand on his forehead. "Why, he's burning with fever!" she exclaimed, turning to her husband. "We'd better call the doctor."

The little fellow tossed and turned. "Me go Sunny Cool?" he begged.

"Not this Sunday, Sonny. Maybe next week," Mother said as she sponged his fevered body and placed cool damp cloths on his forehead. She held him as she rocked in the rocking chair and sang to him, trying to soothe him.

The next day his breathing had become shallow and gasping. He complained of severe pains in his chest. A hacking cough developed, and the coughing spells seemed to tear his little lungs apart.

"He'll get better, won't he?" Mother begged the doctor for reassurance.

"It's going to be a battle," the doctor answered gravely. "A long, hard battle. Pneumonia takes a heavy toll."

Little Albert Dean lost weight rapidly. His eyes became glassy, and his skin took on a transparent look. Night followed day and day followed night. It seemed endless. Mother and Father took turns by the little one's bed soothing him, sponging him, offering him sips of cool water, holding him when the coughing spells racked his body leaving him weak and spent. He seemed to be holding onto life by a mere thread.

And then at last, Mother and Father and Brother Don stood by helplessly and watched the little one slip away in death.

Mother Collins felt it was almost too much to bear. How could she go on? But in time she became aware that her husband and Don were suffering too. She was needed. Don, not quite five years old, needed the security of Mother love and care. She began to busy herself with the needs of the others.

And then one day she learned that a new life was forming within her. "Surely," she said to herself when she felt the child move, "this one has been sent by God to take away the aching void in my heart."

When her time had come and she lay between cool hospital sheets looking at her newborn son lying across her breast, a sigh escaped her lips as her fingers touched the baby's cheek, and then traced around the tiny pink shell-like ear. "This is the child that the Lord has given me to make up for the loss of Albert Dean." A tear trickled down her cheek, but she brushed it quickly away and tried to smile as she looked across at her husband sitting by the bed. She reached out her hand to him and he clasped it in his strong, roughened one.

"What do you think of this one?" Mother Collins asked.

"Oh, he's a fine fellow." Father Collins reached over and touched the baby who had begun to squirm on his mother's breast. "He's a fine fellow!" he repeated. "But how do you feel?"

Now Mother smiled. "Very proud and happy. Just look at his head of hair. He's going to be a redhead, and I'm sure he'll have freckles galore. Takes after your side of the family. He's got a lusty voice too. I can hardly wait until we get home. I wonder how Don will react to his new brother?"

The first time Don saw his tiny red-faced brother, he touched the clenched fist with his finger. The baby stretched, opened one eye and then unclenched his minature fist. Slowly the baby fingers closed around Don's finger.

"Oh, I guess he needs me. He's my brother. My brother Danny." Don grinned up at his parents.

From that day on a special love seemed to grow between the boys. Don spent most of his time near the baby. The next year when he had to go to school, he could hardly wait until time to go home. Dashing into the house, he'd greet Mother and then rush to Baby Danny who would tip back his head and squeal and giggle at sight of his older brother.

As Danny grew older, it was Don who taught him to do the things that boys like to do. How to play special games. How to make whistles. How to climb trees. How to pretend while lying in the grass looking up at the clouds.

When Danny had reached his fourth birthday and Don his ninth, Father Collins received wartime salutations from Uncle Sam, and the induction notice for military service. Because of his family obligations, he was allowed to go into essential industry. He would be placed in the shipyards to work. The family would move to Seattle.

"I can get a job teaching school," Mother said. "I think I could manage to teach school and look after Danny as well. Don will be in school anyway. Danny could play at the back of the schoolroom with crayons and cutouts. We'll need every cent we can get."

Father shook his head slowly. "Well, I don't know—" he paused. "Do you think you could manage the boy and teaching too? It would really help the budget."

"It can be done." Mother smiled. "We'll manage. You'll see."

Mother Collins found a teaching position. Little Danny spent each day in the classroom drawing, coloring, cutting out, and sometimes listening as Mother taught the other children. But before long he became restless.

"Danny, you must be quiet," Mother said. Or, "Danny, please color in your book and leave the children alone. They are studying." Or, "Danny, don't throw the modeling clay around."

"I'm tired," Danny would grumble. "I wanna go outside and play. I don't wanna go to school."

When vacation time came, he tossed his crayons in the air and left the classroom with a skip and a jump and a holler. Free at last. "I hope vacation will never end," he said over and over.

But vacation time did end. It was time for Mother to be back in

the schoolroom—and Danny too. How he hated that. Would that
school year ever end?

The next summer, Danny turned six. "You'll be in the first
grade now," Mother told him.

He squirmed. "Aw, I—I—don't wanna be in the first grade. I
get too tired. I don't wanna even go to school," he whined.

"But you are a big boy now," Mother insisted. "You'll learn to
read and write and—"

"No, I don't wanna." Danny stamped his foot.

But that fall he took his place with the first-graders. However,
he seemed as determined not to like school as Mother was determined that he should learn. Danny, who had already learned the
sound of letters, made faces and poked those around him and
created all sorts of disturbances whenever Mother had her back
turned.

She talked to him. After school she scolded him. She coaxed
him, but to no avail. At the end of the first year Danny had
failed the grade.

"I'll never go back to school." He scowled. "Never!"

One day before the new school year started, Mother Collins put
her arm around Danny. "Sonny," she said, "if you'll take your
first grade over again and pass it, I'll give you five dollars."

"Five dollars!" Danny's eyes shone. "I'll do it."

That year Mother Collins taught the second grade, so Danny
was not in her classroom. He did well the first part of the year,
but before the school year ended the old restlessness had overcome him. But that year he did pass the first grade.

Just before Danny's eighth birthday, Father Collins suggested
that the family move back to New Mexico.

The boys listened while Father and Mother talked over the
idea. They decided to move to Troy. Mother Collins decided not
to teach that school year. She'd give all her time to her family.

As usual summer vacation went all too fast after the family
settled in Troy. Don, now a teen-ager, made friends quickly and
talked a great deal about school; but the nearer opening day
came, the more Danny moped about.

One night Danny overheard his parents talking. "It isn't easy
for children to get started in a new school," Mother Collins said.

"It'll not be so hard on Don. He likes school, makes friends easily, and gets along well with people. But I dread it for Danny. He has such a quick temper, and he hates school."

"I think it is all for the best that you are not teaching this year," Father Collins said. "Sometimes a mother being the teacher gives a boy a disadvantaged feeling. Let's wait and see what happens." Father Collins began to read his newspaper.

That night Danny tossed and turned and slept but little. School again. Why did he have to go to school? If only he could sleep and sleep and sleep and forget to get up!

But suddenly he was being shaken. "Wake up! Come on, wake up! It's time to get going, sleepyhead. First day of school you know."

Danny groaned. "Sure, don't remind me." He opened one eye and then tried to wrap himself up tight in the covers, only to have them jerked away by a grinning brother, Don.

After breakfast, Mother stood at the door and handed the boys their lunch pails. "Be good. Study hard," she said, waving good-bye to them.

Don smiled and waved back, but Danny grunted and scuffed along kicking up puffs of dust.

"Hey, Danny," Don called over his shoulder, "you'll never make it at that snail pace."

"Who cares," Danny retorted. "School again," he sighed. He knew he'd hate it.

He arrived on the school grounds just before the bell rang.

"Hi, Carrottop!" someone yelled.

Danny doubled up his fist. He stuck out his chin belligerently and marched over to a group of boys about his size.

One of the boys looked up from the game of marbles they were playing. "Hey, he'd make a good bean pole," he said with a laugh.

The ringing of the school bell sent the boys scurrying to their places in line. The jostling around of the boys made Danny more angry. "Dummies!" he hissed.

The showdown came after school. When finally he got away from the boys, he hit for home. He slammed the door when he entered the house and stopped for a moment to get his breath.

"Mom! Mom! Where are you?"

"Right here, Danny. I'm sewing."

"I don't ever want to go back to that school," he said, coming to stand in the living room archway.

"Oh, what happened?" Mother's hand flew to her mouth. "Your hair looks like a haystack. Your face is smeared with dirt, and you're missing two buttons on your shirt. And look at your pants!"

Danny's eyes blazed. "It's not me, Mom. It's those mean boys. They call me names. Bean pole! Freckles! Carrottop!" he spat the words out. "It makes me so mad. Why does my hair have to be red? Why do I have so many freckles? I hate it! I hate them!" He slammed his fist against the doorjamb and then shook his injured hand up and down.

"So you've been fighting?" Mother Collins sighed. "Danny, you are always in trouble. Why don't you try to control your temper? There's nothing wrong with having red hair or freckles. You certainly didn't help matters the time you tried to dye your hair with black shoe polish a couple years ago. Remember that? Why, oh why, can't you be like other boys?" Mother paused. "There's a saying that goes something like this: 'Sticks and stones will break my bones, but names will never hurt me.' Say that to yourself, Danny Boy, when someone calls you Bean pole or Freckles or Carrottop."

"I'll try," Danny mumbled.

But time after time Danny came home after school in a rage, his shirt torn, face smeared with grime, hair full of twigs and grass, and scratches on his hands and face.

"The kids just don't like me," he mumbled. "They'd do anything to be mean."

Mother talked and talked to him. Father spent more and more time with him. Don tried to make it easy for him at school by sticking with him more. But Danny hated school. He wanted to be free. Free to roam as he pleased.

"Whatever will happen to you if you go on like this?" Mother Collins despaired as she wiped her eyes. Danny was growing more and more rebellious.

2

The Little Truant

Mother and Father Collins often took their two sons to the movies. Danny looked forward to these times. There was nothing he liked better than going to the movies. One evening, after a particularly interesting show, the family started home in high spirits. Don and Danny ran ahead of their parents acting out some of the comedy parts in their own clownish way. Danny suddenly stopped in the middle of a sentence and pointed. "Look!" There must be a fire. See all the smoke."

They all began to hurry down the road.

"It's our place!" Father Collins shouted and began to run with Mother and the boys following.

When they reached the house, it was in flames. They stood by helplessly watching the flames lick up the roof and walls and all the belongings.

"Our things! Our things are all burned up," Danny wailed.

Father put his arms around his family while the neighbors arrived and offered help.

The next morning, as they searched through the ashes and charred bits of furniture, they found nothing salvageable other than two or three books. "Perhaps the Lord is trying to teach us something," Mother Collins said, looking at the books her husband had picked up. "Whatever do you suppose saved those books from burning?"

"We should be thankful we are safe and together," Father Collins said. "There's nothing for us here." He looked over the ruins.

A few days later he suggested that they move to Chattel, Arizona. "I think we'd have more opportunities there. How about it, Mother?"

"That means another long move," Mother said. "But if you think it is best to go there, we'll go."

Father Collins nodded. "We'll go as soon as school is out."

"Hooray!" Danny shouted. "I'll be glad to leave this school."

That summer Danny and Don began to drift apart. Don, who was five years older, made friends his own age easily. Danny felt left out. Don liked school. Danny couldn't understand how he could stand to be cooped up.

One evening, just before time to start school in the fall, Danny walked into their new home and heard Mother and Father talking. "How I dread for school to start," Mother was saying. Danny stood quietly, unobserved and listened. "I wish Danny loved to study, but he doesn't," Mother went on. "What's worse is that this is a new school again! Children can be so cruel when they don't know each other."

At that, Danny rushed over to Mother. "I don't want to go to school. Please don't make me go."

"Every child has to go to school," Father said firmly while Mother put her arms around Danny. "Come on, Danny," Father went on, "you're a big boy now, and you must go to school. Let's not talk about it anymore."

The first day of school was a nightmare for Danny. He came home in tears. "I don't like that school at all. I won't go back. It's too big. It has that awful fence all around it. I—I just won't go back." His lips quivered. "I—I—I'll be all alone too. Don won't even be able to come home with me."

Mother tried to ignore Danny's outburst. Next morning she

made up special lunches for the boys. She handed them their lunch pails as they left for school. "Have a good day, boys," she called.

They climbed on their bikes and pedaled down the road. Danny lagged farther and farther behind. Don had already crossed the railroad tracks before a long freight train came puffing along. Danny had to brake and stop. The cars rumbled by—car after car after car. Danny knew now he would be late. He stood on one foot and then the other, waiting for the long line of freight cars to pass. He didn't want to go to school, but the thought of being late terrified him.

The last car, the caboose, rumbled by. Danny got on his bike and put on a burst of speed. When he reached the schoolyard, it was empty. He could hear the murmur of voices coming from the open window of one of the classrooms. He stared at the closed door of the schoolhouse.

"I just can't walk into that schoolroom! Everyone will stare at me and teacher'll punish me, and—and it isn't my fault."

Danny turned and pedaled out of the yard. The farther away from school he rode the more frustrated he became. If he went home, Mother would question him. What could he say. What could he do with himself all day? Someone would be sure to see him. Then he became aware of a tall field of corn beside the road. He stopped to admire the waving cornstalks.

"Why not play here until school is out?" the thought came to him. "No one will see me here." He turned his bike off the road, lifted it across a small ditch, and let it lie beside the cornstalks.

All morning Danny played in the cornfield. It was fun not being cooped up in a schoolroom. When he was hungry, he ate his lunch. Then, lying on his back between the rows of tall cornstalks, Danny daydreamed of stalking wild animals in Africa.

"This is great!" He flexed his knees and lifted his head on his hands that had served as his pillow. "When I grow up, I'm going to be a hunter—"

The warm sunshine, his imagination, and the droning of bees and flies must have lulled him to sleep. At the sound of a horn he sat up. He noted that the sun was halfway across the western half of the sky. The school bus rumbled by. Danny jumped up, hopped on his bike, and pedaled for home as fast as possible.

"Hello, Danny boy," Mother greeted him as he came into the yard. "How was school today?"

"OK!" Danny hurried into the house to change his clothes.

The next morning the two boys started off on their bikes again. Danny pedaled slowly, letting Don get far ahead. By the time Danny got across the railroad tracks, Don was out of sight. But there was the cornfield. The stalks seemed to be beckoning. Why should he go to school? No one would miss him. He could stay here and play all day. When the school bus passed, he'd head for home.

Day after day, when he returned home in the afternoon, Mother asked, "How was school today?"

"OK!" he'd say.

"No complaints at all?" Mother looked surprised.

"The kids don't tease me anymore, so it's OK." Danny's heart always beat a little faster with the falsehood.

Three months later, one afternoon while he was in the cornfield, he saw his father's car stop beside the road. Father looked out the window and scratched his head. Then he got out of the car and walked over to Danny's bike. "What's this bike doing here?" he said out loud.

Danny was terrified. He turned to run, but he hadn't gone far when Father overtook him.

"Please, Daddy, don't spank me," he whined as his father held him firmly.

Father said not a word but marched him to the car. He placed the bike in the trunk and then drove home. There Danny sobbed out the whole story. The look on Mother's face added to his misery of being caught.

Next morning, still panic-stricken, Danny whimpered, "Do I have to go to school alone?"

"No, Son, I'll go with you. Then I'll know you are there," Father Collins said.

Together, Danny and Mr. Collins approached the school, Danny hiding a little behind his father.

The teacher stared blankly at Danny when Mr. Collins told her what had happened. "It's been three months," she said. "Your son was here only for registration. Please see the principal."

"How is it you didn't miss my son?" Father asked the principal.

"We simply thought you had moved without notice," the principal said. "I'm sorry, but after all, your son was at school only for registration. I doubt that he can make up his work now."

"We'll see that he studies," Father Collins assured the principal. He left Danny in his assigned classroom and went on his way.

Danny found the day interminable. He couldn't understand the math work. Study as he did at home under Mother's guidance and insistence, he knew he'd never pass the grade that year.

"What's the use?" he'd cry. "I won't pass."

"Well, we're going to try," Mother insisted.

But Danny failed the grade.

That summer Mother Collins received a letter from the schoolboard in Sedan, New Mexico, inviting her to teach there.

"I can get a job in Sedan as well as here," Father said. "Let's go back to New Mexico. That's home."

That first school year in Sedan was one of the few that Danny felt wasn't a complete disaster. The teacher liked him, and he liked the teacher. Here was someone, he realized, who wanted to help him. That year he passed the grade with average marks.

The second year he sensed that his new teacher did not like him. "I'll see that you stop your foolishness, young man," she often said, shaking her long, bony finger at him. And Danny, just as determined, thought to himself, "I'll show her a thing or two!"

That summer Danny spent a lot of time with three of his uncles and his cousin Joe. Mother attended summer school, and Danny stayed at his grandma's house. Danny and Joe ran in and out of Joe's dad's bar. The two cousins learned a lot that summer. The uncles taught and encouraged the two boys to fight and wrestle. And Danny, later that year, got in with a gang of boys who roamed the streets of Sedan looking for trouble.

That school year Danny Collins failed another grade.

"Danny, Danny, what will I do," Mother Collins sobbed, knowing that her son had not only failed another grade but was getting into all sorts of trouble in town. "I just can't face teaching another year. Why is my burden so heavy? Danny, I have always felt that you were sent to me by the Lord."

3

A Stranger at the Door

Mother Collins found that every time a knock came to her door her heart skipped a beat. Would someone be there to tell her that Danny was in some sort of trouble at school or that he had been in a fight or he had been caught playing hooky?

One morning, upon opening the door to a gentle knock, she saw a pleasant-faced, well-dressed woman standing there.

"I'm Mrs. Kiezer, one of your neighbors," the woman said with a smile.

Mother, greatly relieved at seeing the woman, opened the door wide and invited her in.

"I was doing a little neighborly calling this morning," Mrs. Kiezer said, "and since I've not had the privilege of meeting you, I decided to run in this morning. I hope I'm not interrupting anything."

Mother Collins smiled. "No, indeed. I'm glad you came."

They chatted about various things, but soon the conversation took a spiritual turn. "I notice you have a book on your shelf titled *Bible Readings,*" Mrs. Kiezer said, pointing to the book-shelf. "Do you know Seventh-day Adventists?"

"Who?" Mrs. Collins queried.

"Seventh-day Adventists." Mrs. Kiezer replied and explained the meaning of the word.

"Isn't that strange?" Mrs. Collins replied. "I thought only Jews kept the seventh day. That book, *Bible Readings,* we bought from a man selling books in Seattle, Washington, about ten years ago. We also bought that family Bible." She pointed to the Bible on the table. "The book and the Bible were among the very few things salvaged when our home burned. You know, we've never read that book. It's just been left there on the shelf."

Mrs. Kiezer rose to go. "I'd like to come over again," she said. "Would you mind if I brought my husband with me? We could study together from God's Word."

"Why, we'd love that," Mother Collins replied as she took Mrs. Kiezer's hand in hers. "Thank you for dropping by. Why don't you and your husband come over next Tuesday evening?"

It was agreed, and the women parted. Mother Collins went back to her housework with a lightness of heart she had not felt for some time. When her husband came home, she told him about the wonderful neighbor lady who had come to the door. "She and her husband are coming over on Tuesday evening," Mother Collins told him. "We'll study God's Word together."

"OK," Father Collins agreed. "Just remember my family's been Methodists for generations."

When the Kiezers arrived the following Tuesday, Mother ushered them into the living room. "I'm so glad to see you," she said. "Do sit down while I get my husband and the boys."

With her face all smiles, Mother Collins came back to the living room with her companion and Don, a tall handsome fellow in his teens, and Danny. Mother introduced her family to the Kiezers.

After a few minutes of chatting together, Pastor Kiezer showed some pictures and talked about the Word of God. Mother Collins watched the expression on Danny's face.

Father Collins and Danny both insisted that the Kiezers return the following Tuesday evening. And Mother Collins beamed as she said good-night to her new friend.

One evening, after several weeks of study together, Pastor Kiezer said, "This evening we are going to study about death."

Memories that had been carefully set aside flooded Mother Collins's mind. It was hard to grasp all that Pastor Kiezer said that night.

"But I know my little one is in heaven," Mother Collins insisted. "Our minister told me so. I know. I know. It's in the Bible."

Pastor Kiezer smiled. "Well, if it is in the Bible, let's find it," he said. "My wife tells me you have a book—" He turned to the bookshelf. "There it is. This book might be helpful." He walked over to the shelf and took down the book *Bible Readings* and leafed through several pages. Then he handed the open book to Mrs. Collins. "I believe this will help you. God bless you as you study. My wife and I will pray that you find the answer to your question. We'll be over next week." And with that the Kiezers prepared to leave.

Mother Collins began to study the next morning. She kept the book and the Bible beside her a great deal that week. Often she dropped to her knees and pleaded with God to show her the text in the Bible that said her little Albert Dean was in heaven. But her searching and praying seemed in vain.

And then one day she saw it all. "The living know that they shall die: but the dead know not any thing." She read on, "Neither have they any more a portion for ever in any thing that is done under the sun." There were other texts too. Suddenly it all became clear.

As the family gathered for the evening meal, Mother Collins said, "God's Word teaches that the dead do not know anything. That we shall see little Albert Dean on the resurrection morning just as he was when he left us, only in perfect health. Then our family will wing our way to heaven—together."

Father Collins looked up startled. "Here, let me see that!"

Don and Danny looked at each other and shook their heads.

"This does make sense," Father Collins agreed after reading several texts. "I can't refute this."

Later when Pastor Kiezer talked about the seventh day being the true Sabbath, Mrs. Collins bristled. "No," she said firmly.

"We keep the Sunday Sabbath in honor of the resurrection."

Pastor Kiezer again suggested that perhaps it would be well to study further on the topic. "If we should keep Sunday, I surely want to know about it. Is it biblical?"

Mother Collins began to search again.

"Sunday is the Sabbath without a doubt," she said. But search as she did she could not find anything in the Bible to substantiate the idea. At last she realized that the things that were taught in *Bible Readings* were Bible truths.

That Sabbath, the Collinses began attending the Seventh-day Adventist Church with the Kiezers.

"Oh, Daddy," Mother Collins said, tears of joy in her eyes, "at last we are going to church together. How I have longed for this day. I can see God's leadings all along the way."

Father Collins nodded. "I thought I'd never take time for church going. I guess I hoped that you would gain a blessing for all of us, but it didn't work that way, did it?"

That fall Mother and Father Collins planned to be baptized.

"Won't you take your stand with us," Mother urged her two sons.

Don shook his head. "No, not yet. I'm not ready to be baptized. Maybe another time. There are a lot of things I want to do first."

Tears glistened in Mother's eyes. "Oh, Son, don't let the things of the world distract you. I'll be praying for you continually." Then she turned to Danny. "What about you, Danny Boy? Won't you take this step with us? It would make us both so happy."

Danny hung his head.

Mother saw him hesitating. "Please, Danny, give your heart to the Lord."

And at last Danny agreed to be baptized with his parents.

Now things in the family were different. For years they had enjoyed attending movies together. Don still went. Danny, now a member of the church, wanted to go with his older brother, but his parents always said No.

"Why can't I go?" he demanded. "We used to all go and have a good time." Mother Collins tried to explain. She pleaded with Danny to give up the things of the world. Then she went on to explain, "Daddy and I have a commitment to the Lord, Danny. We must abide by that commitment. We cannot give our consent to your moviegoing." She paused and then went on, "It won't be so hard for you if you have young people from the church for your friends. This fall we are going to send you to the church school."

"No!" Danny stormed. "I don't want to go to that little old hick school. All my friends go to the public school. Please don't make me go there."

Father Collins spoke up in a firm tone, "Danny, church school prepares boys and girls for heaven. That is where we want our son to be. We are sending you to church school this fall."

Danny found himself enrolled in the church school in the fall. He was determined not to enjoy it. He was determined to make it hard for the teachers as well.

"Danny, we do not use that kind of language here," the teachers daily admonished.

"Danny, we don't read that type of thing here," they said over and over when they found him reading comic books or trying to get others to read them.

One day he brought his .22 to school. "Hey, let's play cops and robbers," he shouted on the playground.

The schoolboard met. Should Danny be expelled for insubordination? He was certainly not a good influence on the other students. Half the board members thought Danny should be expelled. The others said, "Let's give him another chance. You know his mother is a wonderful woman. For her sake let's give him another chance."

So Danny was allowed to remain at school. He even passed from the seventh to the eighth grade.

"Do I have to go back to that school next term?" he asked when school was out.

"Let's not worry about it now." Mother put him off.

That summer Mother and Father Collins talked about and prayed for their two sons earnestly. By this time Don had finished high school and had a job. But Danny was still under their care. If only they could keep him in church school, surely the influence of Christian boys and girls and Christian teachers would rub off on their wayward son.

At last Father Collins decided to bargain with him. "If you'll go to church school another year, Son, I'll let you drive the family car to school."

"Really? You mean it?" Danny, now a teen-ager showed interest. "OK! It's a bargain."

"Just remember that driving a car is a responsibility," Father admonished.

"I know! I know! You can count on me. I won't drive fast, and I'll obey all the rules."

But Danny's love of showing off, his unruly temper, his association with rough town boys and his occasional moviegoing, got him into trouble. That school year, after only a few months, he was dismissed from church school.

Once more Danny went to the public school. He began to smoke and drink heavily. He was suspended from school several times that year and finally placed under the control of a probation officer who ordered him to attend school faithfully.

"If you cause any more problems, you'll be placed immediately in a reform school," the probation office warned.

4

Sowing Wild Oats

"You know, Dad, if I had a car of my own, everything would be different," Danny said as he and his father stood looking at the family car, not of modern vintage and in need of a tune-up. "If you'd get me a car of my own, I promise to be real careful."

Father Collins looked Danny right in the eye. "Seems to me you've made similar promises when I let you have the family car."

"Dad, this time I really mean to keep my promise. I'll do differently. I'll make a change in my life."

For a few moments Father Collins didn't answer. Then he said, "Well, you are seventeen now. You ought to be settling down. OK, I'll see about getting a car for you."

They found a car in a used car lot that Danny decided was the one for him. Dad paid for it and handed him the keys with the words, "Remember, driving is a great responsibility."

But now Danny had another problem. His friends were hesitant to ride with him. Their parents were not happy with Danny's wild ways and his driving. But there were always older boys who didn't have a car, and Danny learned that they were always eager to go places. And Danny was always willing and eager to oblige and take a dare.

Danny and his car were well known to the highway patrol. He was always getting a ticket. Then he learned some tricks to keep from being caught. It got to be a real joke with him—his ability to outmaneuver the traffic officers.

At home he came and went as he pleased. He knew he was difficult and often belligerent. But his mother never seemed to give up on him. No matter what hour of the night he came home there was always a glass of milk and a sandwich on his bedside table. Many a night when he passed Mother's bedroom with the door slightly ajar he heard her praying out loud for him.

One night, when Danny came home unusually late, his mother came into his room.

"Please, Mother, leave me alone. I don't want a lecture. You always seem to be spying on me," he grumbled.

"I've been praying for you, Danny Boy," she said quietly.

"Well, I don't need your prayers. Just let me alone!" He flung the words out angrily.

He heard Mother gasp. He turned to see her clutch at her heart and then walk unsteadily from the room. Suddenly his eyes filled with tears. He felt choked. Why had he lashed out like that. Mother had always been so good to him. But he brushed the tears away and tried to reassure himself. "Mother's just being dramatic. And I'm doing all right."

But the next few days Mother stayed in bed. When Danny came home one afternoon, he found the family doctor at the house with Father Collins. Father motioned Danny into the living room and closed the door. "Your mother is sick, Danny. She's going to need a lot of rest and quiet and no worry."

"Danny," the doctor spoke up, "if you don't change your ways, you are going to kill your mother. You are breaking her heart."

He didn't want to listen to any lecturing just then. What were they trying to do, scare him? He hurried out of the house and got into his car and drove off. As he pulled onto the highway, he recognized two of his buddies in another car. He honked his horn and passed them. The other car drew up alongside. Then they began to race down the highway. Most of the time the cars raced side by side. Suddenly Danny saw an oncoming car. It was almost upon them. Where had it come from? He felt confused. He swerved his car and went into the ditch. There was a sickening crash! Danny knew the two cars had hit head on.

He heard voices. But he seemed unattached to it all—as if he were floating. Then sharp, searing pain slashed at him. There was the sound of a siren that seemed to split the air and Danny's head too. He knew no more until he awoke in a hospital bed.

"What—what happened?" he asked groggily.

"There was an accident. Now just rest. You'll learn more about it when you feel better," a nurse told him.

Unconsciousness overcame him again.

"Two cars! There were two cars. I heard the crash. What happened?" The memory began to take shape in his mind when he regained consciousness.

At last they told him. The driver of the oncoming car was badly injured, and two young fellows on their way back to the Adventist academy at Corrales had been killed.

It took awhile for it to sink in—that two boys had been killed! And then a heavy feeling of guilt settled on him. It had all been his fault. He had challenged his friends to a race. If that hadn't happened, the two boys would even now be back at the academy. But he, Danny, had been the cause of their deaths. He groaned.

Of course there would be a trial. Danny knew that he was in real trouble. He went over and over his past. He'd surely receive a sentence of some kind. He'd been warned to keep out of trouble. He'd deserve whatever sentence he got. But he didn't want to go to reform school.

At last the time came when Danny stood before the judge. There were the district attorney, the chief of police, other police officers, and his probation officer. He felt sick and scared. He watched the judge flip through a stack of papers. Could those all be charges against him?

Finally the judge cleared his throat. He looked straight at Danny, leaning forward at the bench as he did so. "Young man," he said, "the company you are keeping, your lack of interest in school, in short, the kind of life you are leading—all of these have already got you into serious trouble. An education is important. Obedience to laws and discipline are important." He paused. "I want to discuss this matter further with the probation officer. I think a reform school is the best place for you. You've got to settle down or else. You've had warnings and chances before, but they haven't helped."

Danny hung his head. "Please, your honor, don't send me to a reform school." Although almost eighteen years old, Danny couldn't keep the tears from gathering in his eyes. His voice trembled. "My folks have been wanting me to go to an Adventist academy. They've been talking about sending me to Sandia View Academy. It's run by the Seventh-day Adventist Church. They've got very strict rules. I'd be working half days and going to school the other half. My parents would be happy if I went to Sandia View Academy. I've been balking at the idea, but—but—" As if the idea just came to him, he looked up at the judge and said, "If anyone gets the credit for straightening me out, I—I—want it to be God."

The judge's eyes seemed to pierce through Danny. Then he motioned the probation officer to step up to the bench. They talked together in low tones, while Danny shifted uneasily from one foot to the other.

The probation officer finally returned to his place. The courtroom was absolutely silent. Danny stood there feeling as if he had already been condemned. At last the judge spoke.

"Young man, the court has decided that something has to be done to change your way of life."

There was a pause. Danny's heart raced. It was reform school for him, for sure.

"This court has decided," the judge continued slowly as if weighing each word, "that you shall be sent to—to—that Seventh-day Adventist academy provided your father will pay the bill."

A subdued Danny left the court with his father who had promised to send him to Sandia View Academy.

The arrangements with the academy were made, and Danny found himself enrolled at the Adventist school. There were a few students he knew from his church school days, but they seemed aloof, not ready to be friends with Danny.

"Do they think I'll contaminate them?" Danny asked one of the students who befriended him.

"Aw, they're sissies. Who needs them," the boy replied. "I'll introduce you to some real fellows." He winked at Danny.

It wasn't long until Danny found himself surrounded by a group of boys, rough in speech and action. Little by little Danny became more and more involved with these friends who cared little for spiritual values and who seemed bent on breaking rules and causing the faculty much concern.

One thing led to another, and one day the dean called Danny aside. "You know, Danny," he said firmly but kindly, "your days at Sandia View are numbered if your attitudes and your choice of companions don't change. You know the consequences, Danny, if you are expelled from Sandia View."

Danny knew the consequences well. He determined to be more careful. But little by little his old habits and his old friends got to him. "Of course," he reasoned, "I'll watch my steps closely from now on."

But the day came when the dean called him to the office and Danny knew the reason why. Reform school loomed up in his imagination. He sat with his head bowed while the dean spoke.

"I'm sorry, Danny. The whole faculty is sorry, but we have no choice but to dismiss you from the school. We are sending a letter to your parents telling them of our decision, and why. You will remain at the academy and on the campus until your parents arrange for your return home. We will turn your car keys over to your parents."

Danny rushed from the dean's office. Anger, and fear of the future were mixed. Hurrying into his room at the dorm he slammed his fist into the pillow on the bed as he flung himself down. Then he sat up defiantly. "I'm not waiting for anything. Good thing they don't know about the extra set of car keys I didn't turn in. They can't keep me here. I'm leaving." He pulled out a suitcase from under the bed and began throwing his things into it. While the students were at dinner in the cafeteria, Danny piled his things in the car and started home.

Mother greeted him with open arms. "Oh, Danny Boy, it's so

good to see you. I had no idea you had a break this month. Come on and have some good home cooking," she urged.

An hour later word came from the academy, Danny was missing. He had been expelled, the principal told Mother over the phone. Danny knew what it was all about by the look on Mother's face while she listened. When she replaced the receiver, she went into her bedroom without saying a word.

Danny waited and waited for Mother to come out of her room. The clock on the wall ticked away the minutes as Danny waited. At last he could stand it no longer. He went to the door and listened. He couldn't hear a sound—not even the sound of weeping. He remembered how Mother had prayed for him. He thought of how happy she had been when he had gone to the academy and her joy at his homecoming that she had assumed was because of a school break. What a blow it must have been to find out that he had been expelled. He had to go in to her. He wanted her to know that he loved her. Danny turned the knob and opened the door slightly.

There Mother lay on the bed, her face drained of color. Her lips contorted in pain while her hands, those hands that Danny knew had done so much for him, clutched at her breast.

"Your heart! Is—is—it your heart, Mom?" Danny rushed over to the bed and dropped to his knees beside it. "What shall I do? Mother! Mother!" he sobbed. Who could help him?

He rushed out of the room. "Who should I call?" he groaned. And it was then he looked up. "Oh, God," he cried, "forgive me. I'm sorry for all my mistakes. Please save my mother. Give me another chance. I promise I'll give myself to You if You'll just save my mother's life. I'll do anything You want me to do. Anything—"

He went back into the bedroom. Mother was dead!

A voice within him said, "You've killed her! You've killed her!"

Danny lashed out, "Why didn't God save my mother? It's all the fault of that school. They had no right to dismiss me like that. I—I promised God I'd do anything if He'd save Mother. He didn't. What's the use?" Danny was inconsolable.

To blur his conscience he began to drink heavily. Soon having committed a felony while under the influence of liquor, Danny found himself in court again.

"Have you anything to say for yourself?" the judge asked.

Danny looked up at the judge. "Yes, your honor, I would like to try to make something of myself. I would like the opportunity to join one of the armed services."

The judge hesitated. He looked over the top of his glasses. "Well, the penitentiary isn't going to do you much good, but the armed services just might." He seemed deep in thought as he studied Danny.

"All right," he said at last, "which will it be? The Marines, the Navy, the Army, or the Air Force? We'll give you a chance to make up your mind."

A Marine sergeant was called in to interview Danny. A court officer told him all about Danny's problems.

"This is the kind of man we like," the sergeant said. "You've got to be tough to join the Marines. We'll straighten him out."

A Navy man was called in next. He looked over Danny's long record. "If we can't handle him, we'll march him down the gangplank and leave him out at sea."

The prospect of going to sea didn't appeal to Danny at all. The Navy wasn't what he wanted. He was sure the Army wouldn't want him because they did a great deal of marching, and an old injury to his knee made marching impossible.

"Well, have you made up your mind?" the judge asked. Then he added, "Or do you want to try the Army or the Air Force?"

"The Air Force, sir," Danny mumbled.

The Air Force officer read the long list of charges. He tapped the sheet with his pencil. "We don't usually take anyone with a record like yours. We want fellows with a clean record and at least a high school education. You've got a lot of marks against you."

Danny's heart sank.

But the officer continued, "How do you feel about it? Do you really want to learn a skill that you can use later in civilian life? Fortunately you're young yet. We'll take you, young man, if you will apply yourself. Do you really want to learn? If this isn't what you want, we don't want you. It's as simple as that."

"I'll join the Air Force, your honor," Danny's voice was muffled.

The judge leaned forward and cupped his hand around his ear.

3—M.S.D.

"Speak up, young man, speak up."

"The Air Force, your honor."

The judge sat back. "Remember this, young man, if you receive a dishonorable discharge, don't show up in this town again. Case dismissed." He tapped his gavel sharply on the desk.

5

In the Air Force

Within a few days Danny found himself in the United States Air Force. His hair was cropped short. He wore fatigues, the same as every other enlisted person. His identity seemed to have been stripped from him. Here there was no privacy. His life was ruled by commands and schedules. The exercising, the endless routines, the orders barked at the men, left him at the end of the day bone weary and drained. Never in his life had he felt so alone— alone among so many strangers. Homesick? Why should he be homesick? This had been his choice. Besides, he had no home now. Mother was gone.

Mother! How often he thought of her and all the things she had done for him. How ungrateful he had been. Yes, he had killed her. He had broken her heart. Danny wanted to cry out in his loneliness and grief, but he was no longer Mother's Danny Boy. He was now Private Dan Collins, U.S. Air Force. No one, he determined, would ever know how he felt inside. And Dan made himself known to his buddies as one of the toughest.

For the first two weeks of his training he stood each day at mail-call time with the other fellows waiting for mail. His name was never called.

"Well, what could I expect," he mumbled as he made his way back to the barracks and sat down on his cot, head in hands. He knew that all around him fellows were reading letters from friends and loved ones. But who would write to him? Mother would have written. Of that he was sure. But Mother was dead. And again the searing thought came; he was responsible.

What was the use of going to mail call. No one would write. Dad was too broken up over Mother's death. Dad, too, he felt, blamed him for what had happened.

"Well, I am responsible," he said. "It was all my fault."

But the next day he did go to mail call. He stood nonchallantly at ease. One after another his buddies stepped forward to receive their mail.

"Dan Collins!" the corporal's voice rang out.

Dan's heart began to pound. He looked around, not sure he had heard right.

"Collins, Dan Collins," the corporal barked again.

Dan stumbled forward. He righted himself and reached out for the mail.

The corporal placed a package in his outstretched hand.

Dan's hands trembled. He wanted to turn and run and shout. He also felt a lump in his throat that seemed to choke him. He had to get out of the mob. Who could be sending him a package? Was it a joke? A cruel joke? He turned the package over. He shook it. Well, why wait? Dan tore off the wrapping. There lay a note on top of two books.

"Dear Dan," the note read. "We wish you a happy time in the service. We love you."

"Presented by the Clayton Seventh-day Adventist Church.

"Sincerely,

"Mrs. C. V. Coulton."

And there beneath the card were a small Bible and the little book, *Steps to Christ*.

Dan felt as if he'd been hit with a ton of bricks. He read the card again and again to make sure he had read correctly. It was hard to swallow. He felt tears in his eyes. He brushed his sleeve across his tear-wet eyes. No one but Mother had ever shown an interest in his spiritual well-being before. But she was gone. And he, Dan, had been the cause. That thought kept coming back again and again. Why had the church back home bothered to remember him. He'd let the folks know that he had no use for them. But here was the note and the books. He had to get out of this mob. He roughly shoved his way past the other men and went to his barracks. He didn't want the boys to know that he had received these books, a Bible and *Steps to Christ*. He had to keep up his reputation of being one of the toughest in the outfit.

Going over to his cot and whistling a bawdy tune, Dan kicked his foot locker and then stopped whistling long enough to let out an oath. Then, lifting the lid of the locker, he placed the Bible and the book in it and slammed the lid shut.

Three days later he took the book from its hiding place. He had nothing to do that night. He might as well leaf through it. There was a picture of Christ praying in the Garden of Gethsemane. Dan stared at the picture. Then he quickly turned to the back of the book and read the verse at the close of the chapter.

The thought of Mother came to him again. He lay there on his cot, the little book open, when one of the fellows interrupted his thoughts with a loud guffaw. "Hey, Collins! what kind of dirty book are you reading this time?"

Dan sprang up from his cot. His face flushed crimson. He clenched his fists. One of the few times in his life he'd been looking at something worthwhile, and this fellow asked what dirty book he was reading! Dan's first impulse was to give the fellow a good thrashing. Then he wondered why he got so angry. Why hadn't he made a simple retort. He was much surprised to hear himself saying, "OK. I'm going to read to you from this book. And let me tell you I don't want a single one of you to interrupt. Understand?"

He turned back to the first chapter. Then he looked around the room. Practically every fellow in the room was looking at him. He began to read in an icy tone of voice. He'd show these guys! He read the first page, and the second, and the third. There was not a sound in the room, but Dan's voice reading the chapter "God's

Love for Man" from the little book *Steps to Christ*. The coldness had left his voice. The words now came out warm and full of meaning. Dan read on and on. He read until the lights went out. Then he tucked the book under his pillow.

The men prepared for bed quietly that night. The one who had made the remark to Dan earlier in the evening came over to his cot. "That's a good book," he said, shifting his weight uneasily from one foot to the other and looking down at the floor.

"Uh-huh!" Dan grunted a dismissal.

The next day no one mentioned the reading of the night before. But that evening the young man spoke up: "Say, Collins, are you going to read to us again?"

Dan waited to hear the others laugh or make some remark. He'd never been asked to do anything like that before. There was no laughter. The fellows all seemed to be waiting for his answer.

He pulled the book from under his pillow. As he held it in his hand, the experiences of the past seemed to flash before him— Mother urging him to become a Christian; Mother loving him through all his willfulness; his wild associations, his academy days; the events that led up to his joining the Air Force. Now there was no fight left in him.

The men seemed to be waiting. There was no laughing or joking. Dan opened the book and began to read again. As he read, he began to realize something within him pointing up a great need. He knew he wanted to have a better life. He wanted Jesus to take control. He wanted to be a follower of Christ. He felt the need to commit his ways to Christ. "But how does one make a commitment?" He puzzled.

Dan had not attended church in a long time. He had not heard of a church near the base. Down deep inside he knew something was happening to him.

At last he decided to write to his father and tell him of his new determination, the determination to live every day for the Lord. He also told his father he wanted to come home on his first leave.

A week later Dan received an answer to the letter he had written. "I'll meet you at the bus depot, Son. How wonderful it will be to have you home with me for a few days."

It was on a Friday when Dan took the bus for home. He looked forward to going to church with his father on the Sabbath. How his heart beat faster as the bus neared his hometown. He swung down the moment the bus stopped. There was his father. The two men rushed to each other and embraced.

"Hi, Dan!"

"Hi, old buddy!"

Dan heard the voices behind him and turned to see several of his old associates standing on the platform.

"Come on, Danny, let's have a drink. We've brought a whole case to celebrate," one of the boys said, slapping him on the shoulder.

"Have we got plans!" another grinned at him. "It's good to see ya' back."

Dan turned to his father. He saw the hurt look on his face, but he didn't say a word.

"You go home, Dad. I'll be there shortly," Dan said, and watched his father with stooped shoulders turn and walk away.

He'd tell the fellows he didn't drink anymore. He'd stay only a little while. Then he'd go home and get ready for the Sabbath. He would attend the church where Mother had attended—the church that had sent him the Bible and *Steps to Christ.*

With much laughing and back slapping and off-color joking the fellows pushed Dan along to a bar. They didn't seem to notice at first that Dan simply held a glass in his hand.

But soon one of the fellows, already a little drunk, came over to Dan and sneered, "What'sa matter, you not drinking?"

The fellow sitting next to Dan then put his face close to Dan's and in a slurred voice said, "You got ideas of bein' better'n us?"

Dan laughed nervously. He put the glass to his lips and took a sip. He didn't want to have the boys think he felt superior. He took another and then another.

He went home late that night, sloppy drunk.

Next morning Dan groaned as he lifted his head from the pillow and then fell back. What a hangover! It slowly dawned on him that this was the Sabbath. The day he had looked forward to—to going to church with his dad. He couldn't go in this condition. Remorse swept over him. In fact, how could he ever go to church after what he had done. What was the use? "I'm no good. What's the use of trying. I've sure made a mess of my life." Dan buried his head in the pillow.

Somehow he managed to see the time. He knew then that Dad had gone to church without him. Dad had found him drunk! Dan was overcome with remorse. He couldn't stay here. Not after what he'd done. Dan struggled out of bed and packed his few belongings and left the house while Dad was still at church. He felt sure that Dad would never trust him now and would surely never want to see him again.

He hurried to the bus station and got a bus back to the base.

A few days later his first orders came through. He was to be stationed in Iceland!

Dan left the States almost immediately. He had not written to his father, nor had his father written him. He felt sure that his father was through with him. He had failed in his commitment to Christ. There was no use in trying. And Dan began to drink heavily again.

Dan had plenty of time in Iceland to see the sights, and he thoroughly enjoyed his work at the Icelandic base out of the city of Reykjavik. He and one of his buddies, Cliff Brown, often traveled to the city where they partied and drank and played cards. But down deep inside, Dan had a longing for something different.

One day, upon coming into his barracks he found some magazines on his cot—*Signs of the Times, Review and Herald,* and *The Youth's Instructor.* "Now, whoever sent me these?" Not wanting to be teased about having church papers, he pushed them under his mattress, slipping them away out of sight.

On his next leave, Dan went to Europe. He forgot about the magazines he had laid aside, but upon his return there they were on his bed with several new ones that had been opened. Things that he had wanted to hide were out in the open for everyone to see.

He picked up a magazine and looked at the cover picture. Then he turned it over. On the back page was a sort of emblem with a white star in the center and the words: "Seventh-day Adventists in Iceland are the same the world over."

"Seventh-day Adventists in Iceland!" He spoke out loud. He'd inquired about an Adventist Church when he'd first arrived and had been told there was none. There wasn't even a Seventh-day Adventist chaplain in the Air Force. "That's not a true state-ment," he said pushing the papers aside again.

"Say, Cliff," Dan confided to his friend one day when they planned to go to Reykjavik for a weekend party, "I'd like to find a certain church in the city, a Seventh-day Adventist Church." He paused. "I used to attend that church when I was a kid in the States," he said. "You know, of all the churches, that Adventist bunch are about the best." Then he pulled out the magazines and showed Cliff the magazine with the statement "Seventh-day Adventists in Iceland are the same the world over."

"Come on. Are you ready?" Cliff asked, interrupting Dan. The two stuffed their large whiskey flasks in the pockets of their greatcoats and then set out.

"Let's see if we can find an Adventist church in the city," Dan suggested.

"OK," Cliff agreed. "Where will we look first, the police station?"

Dan shrugged. "Why not. That seems a good place to start."

But when they inquired at the police station, the man in charge told them he had never heard of a Seventh-day Adventist church.

"Wait! Wait a minute," a man standing nearby walked up to the boys. "Do you mean *Adventistar?*"

"I guess I do," Dan agreed.

The man gave directions.

So there was an Adventist Church in Iceland. Dan's heart beat faster as they approached the street where they had been di-rected.

"What are you going to do when you get there?" Cliff asked.

Dan laughed. "Well, I'll tell you what. If the church is open, I'll go in and you can go on to the party."

"You expect to find the church open at this hour?" Cliff raised his eyebrow.

"There it is!" Dan pointed as they turned a corner. "See the sign. I know enough of the language to know that that sign says it is an Adventist church. He started up the stairs two at a time, reaching back to draw Cliff along. He could hear singing. Suddenly the door opened and two men stepped outside as if barring the entrance.

"Is this a Seventh-day Adventist Church?" Dan asked. *"Adventistar?"*

The men nodded.

"Well, may we come in?" Dan motioned to the door and took a step forward. Then he noticed that the two men seemed to be looking down at his bulging greatcoat pocket.

"Oh, I don't intend to take this inside." He reached for the flask in his pocket, pulled it out and handed it to Cliff. "See you later," he said, waving a hand toward his friend.

Cliff hurried down the church steps.

The men opened the door, and Dan entered the little Adventist church. The singing was beautiful. He couldn't understand the words, but he recognized the music. He learned that an evangelistic meeting was in progress. "Too bad," he thought, "I won't be able to understand a word." But much to his amazement the evangelist stepped to the podium and spoke in English. His message was translated to the four hundred Icelanders there.

It couldn't have been just chance that the papers had been left on his cot! The papers with the emblem and the words: "Seventh-day Adventists in Iceland are the same the world over." No, he felt certain he had been guided here to this place. Once more he felt God's Spirit talking to him, and he determined to become a true Seventh-day Adventist and go to church each Sabbath morning.

He had made a decision. When he returned to the base, he spoke to the sergeant. "Sir, I wish to keep the seventh day holy. I would like the privilege of attending church on each Saturday."

The sergeant stared at him. "Are you crazy. This is the Air Force. That's impossible."

"Sir," Dan said quietly, "I request to see the commanding officer."

The sergeant finally took Dan to see the commanding officer. After saluting and some preliminary talk, the sergeant said, "Do you think this fellow needs to go to church?"

The commanding officer looked Dan up and down. "Well, he

needs something. If it would do him any good, fine. If it does him no good, then I say, No."

Dan realized that the two men were making fun of him. He noticed the commanding officer wink at the sergeant. He then said, "Do you suppose there might be a girl at church he wants to see?"

Dan spoke up quickly. "Sir, I really want to go to church. If you permit me to go, I will bring back a program for you to see each week. That will prove to you that I have been there."

There was complete silence in the room. The commanding officer seemed to have forgotten him. But at last he spoke to the sergeant.

"OK, sergeant, give this man a pass for Saturdays for one month. We'll try him out and see if going to church helps him any."

6

Failure

Although he could understand but little of the services in the Adventist Church in Reykjavik, Dan attended every Sabbath, and he enjoyed being with his newfound friends. He knew that Adventists were a temperate people; they neither drank nor smoked, and he knew they were very careful about the language they used. He knew about the Sabbath. He felt the kinship of these Adventists in Reykjavik. He longed for a deeper and fuller relationship with Christ.

Dan wrote to his father telling him about his renewed stand for Christ, and the joy he had in fellowship with Christians in Reykjavik. He told his father how he longed to come home for a visit and share his future hopes and plans. He was sorry for his actions at the time of his last homecoming. This time things would be different.

At last the time came and the orders received that Dan could go home on furlough. He wrote his father at once telling him of his arrival time. Eagerly Dan counted the hours until he would be reunited with his father and the people in the little church where his mother had attended.

There was Father Collins on the station platform. Dan saw him scanning every passenger that alighted from the coach. At last he swung down. Father's eyes lighted up. In an instant, the two embraced.

"Let me look at you, Son. You're a sight for sore eyes," Father Collins said, grasping Dan's arms and holding him at arm's length.

Dan saw tears in his father's eyes. Tears of joy, he knew. His own eyes felt moist too, as he placed his arm around dad's shoulders. "It's been so long," he said.

Dan didn't see the roistering group of fellows until they surrounded him and his father, so interested had he been in meeting once more this man whom he had let down a few years before.

"Well, old buddy, we got wind that you were coming in," one of the fellows said.

"Good to see ya, man!" from another.

"Thanks," Dan replied, offering a handshake, a slap on the back to each of the half-tipsy men. He turned to his father. "I better send them off," he said in a half-embarrassed way. "You better leave them to me. I'll be home shortly. Don't worry."

The fellows laughed and pushed Dan ahead of them, leaving Father Collins standing alone on the platform.

Dan turned once and got a glimpse of him, shoulders stooped. A hurt, worried look had taken the place of the joy of meeting. But Dan only saw him for a moment and the boys closed in on him and hurried him off.

At first their off-color jokes and drinking bothered Dan. This wasn't the kind of life he'd been enjoying lately. But then they complained that he wasn't like he used to be. He was a sissy. The Air Force had made a pantywaist out of him. He laughed and little by little yielded to their urgings to drink and enjoy life.

Dan knew little of how or when he got home that night. The next morning despondency swept over him. He had come home to be with his father and share his newfound joy of being a Christian. And here he was, his head splitting, his mouth tasting musty and foul, his stomach queasy—everything seemed so useless. How could he have been so thoughtless of his father? How could he have let his Lord down? He couldn't face his father? He was defeated. It was just no use for him to try. He couldn't stand on his own two feet.

Dan argued with himself. "I want to be a Christian. I've been praying a lot about it. But I'm just no good. Oh, why do I fail? I thought the Lord would give me power. But here I am a miserable failure again."

The remaining days of Dan's leave were like a nightmare. He returned to the base as soon as possible. He couldn't face the people at the church. He couldn't stand to see his father's hurt, bewildered look.

"If only I could stand up for what I know is right—" he moaned.

Dan's next orders were to report to an Air Force base in North Carolina. The gnawing pain in his heart seemed intolerable. He decided to put in a request for a discharge. But he received no reply. At last Dan found an Adventist chaplain, a Pastor Walmont. He poured out his story to the chaplain, sparing nothing.

When he had finished speaking, the chaplain said quietly, "Dan, just leave the past with the Lord. What counts now is what you do with your life today. The Lord says, 'If we confess our sins, he is faithful and just to forgive us our sins, and to cleanse us from all unrighteousness.' He has said it, Dan. Do you believe it? He also says that as far as the east is from the west so far will He remove your sins from you. Do you believe it?"

Dan sat with his head down.

"Those are not my words, but Christ's. Do you believe it, Dan?" Chaplain Walmont asked again.

Dan sat up straight. "Thank you, sir," he said.

"Just thank the Lord day by day," Chaplain Walmont said, rising to his feet. "Thank Him for what He has done and for what He can and will do for you. Remember, He 'was in all points tempted like as we are.' Another text says, 'There hath no temptation taken you but such as is common to man: but God is faithful, who will not suffer you to be tempted above that ye are able; but will with the temptation also make a way to escape, that ye may be able to bear it.' Dan, do you believe it?" Chaplain Walmont asked again.

"Yes, sir," Dan stood to his feet and grasped the chaplain's hand. "I believe it!"

The next day Dan went to his sergeant. "Sir," he said, "I am a Seventh-day Adventist Christian. I cannot bear arms. I should like your permission to—"

"Collins," the sergeant snapped, "you're in the Air Force. Every man has to bear arms in this branch of the service. Who do you think you are? You'd better be ready to report tomorrow."

"I am sorry, sir, I cannot be there," Dan replied.

"That's an order, Collins. That's an order. You be there!" the sergeant barked.

The next morning Dan returned to the office. The sergeant looked up from his desk.

"Collins, we may not make you use a gun, but we'll make you wish you had," he said in a sneering tone of voice.

Anger swept over Dan. Forgetting where he was and to whom he was speaking he leaned across the desk and said, "All right, sarg, if you're going to do it, let's get on with it."

The sergeant leaped to his feet. His face contorted with rage. "I could have you court-martialed for this. Report immediately to the woodwork shop. We'll teach you a thing or two. So, you're a Christian, are you?"

Dan's face blanched. He'd said he was a Christian. But he'd certainly not acted like one. He'd failed again. But the words flashed through his mind: "If we confess our sins, he is faithful and just to forgive." Dan sent up a silent prayer for forgiveness and help. Then he turned and left the office.

At the woodwork shop Dan was ordered to keep the equipment free from dust. He noticed the men at work winked at each other as he whisked dust from the machinery. But as soon as he'd wipe the dust away there would be more dust again caused by the continual planing and sawing of the lumber that went on and on.

The inspector kept dogging his footsteps. "Get back there, Collins, don't you see the dust?" he'd growl.

"Yes, sir! Yes, sir!" Collins would run back and go over the same machine again.

There were times when a surly retort almost slipped from his lips. But no, he was a Christian. The Lord would and could help him. Dan began to realize that this time spent dusting the machines in the shop was meant for his good. He was learning to rely on a higher power. He was learning that of himself he could do nothing, but all things were possible to those who believe and trust.

Day after day Dan reported for his work—dusting machinery. Day after day he listened to the ridicule of the men and the commands of the inspector. Day after day he learned to trust in the Lord for help and calmness of spirit.

At the end of the month Dan was ordered to report for K.P. duty.

He was told that if he reported by 4:00 a.m. he would be able to pick his job. Dan arrived to report at 3:30.

Much to his astonishment everyone else was assigned a job first. Dan was finally ordered to wash the pots and pans.

"Sir, I was here first," Dan spoke up politely.

"Orders from headquarters," the officer of the day said.

Dan set to work. The kettles stacked up around him. He washed as fast as he could, but he couldn't seem to get to the bottom of the pile. Perspiration dripped from his forehead. His hands felt raw from the scouring and the hot water. Just when he thought he was at last catching up, the officer in charge would toss back a well-washed kettle with the order: "Collins, this kettle needs more polishing."

Dan worked all day until five in the evening. From eight to five, five days a week. At the end of the work day he went to his barracks completely exhausted. For thirty days Dan scrubbed pots and pans, and daily prayed for patience and strength.

At the end of Dan's K.P. service, the sergeant called him into the office. "Collins," he said, "I understand you want out of the service. We'll give you a general discharge."

"Is that an honorable discharge, sir?" Dan asked.

"After six months," the sergeant replied, leaning back on the two back legs of the chair and staring at Dan.

"If the discharge is not an honorable one, I don't want it."

The sergeant let the chair come to rest on all four legs with a thud. He grabbed the front of the desk. "If you behave yourself, it will be honorable in six months."

Dan stammered, "But—but, sir, I have been behaving myself, sir."

The sergeant spoke up coldly: "If you will not take a general discharge, we'll give you a dishonorable one."

"Dishonorable? Sir, dishonorable for what?"

The sergeant began to write something on a slip of paper. Then he motioned to a corporal. "Put this man on the clean-up crew." He turned to Dan. "Dismissed!"

Dan followed the corporal.

His new assignment was to walk down the road and pick up cigarette butts. However, as he walked along picking up thrown-away butts, it seemed someone was always following him dropping butts.

"Collins, why don't you do your work right? Get back here and pick up the rest of these butts," he was constantly harangued.

And Dan would rush back. "Yes, sir! Yes, sir!" He was surprised at himself for his calmness and for not retorting back.

"Thank You, Father," he prayed, knowing that it was only by God's power that he was able to keep from fighting or cursing at the unfair treatment. How thankful he was when the Sabbath day came and he could attend the Seventh-day Adventist Church with Chaplain Walmont. The chaplain and all the church members prayed for him daily.

Once more Dan was ordered back to the woodwork shop; then he was ordered to the commissary to unload hundred-pound sacks of potatoes from trucks that brought provisions to the base.

One day he was taken to the commanding officer's headquarters. "Collins," the officer barked, "Do you see this tile?" He pointed to the dull looking tile floor. "I want the wax stripped off until this tile is as white as the tile in the hall. Do you understand?"

Dan set to work. He stripped the tile five times but it still had a yellowish tinge. He felt sure that the officer was trying to trip him up. With a happy heart, Dan realized that the Holy Spirit had been with him to sustain him. And he began to realize fully that all things do work together for good. The officer began to praise him for his good work. One of the majors told the sergeant who had been unkind to him to "lay off Collins, he's OK."

4—M.S.D.

While cleaning off one of the desks, Dan opened a drawer to drop in some pencils. There he noticed his name on a sheet of paper. Since it was on top of everything, he read the words "Honorable Discharge!" There it was. He had an honorable discharge from the United States Air Force.

However, when Dan was informed of the discharge, the officers urged him not to leave. This puzzled him.

"Everything is going OK for you, why leave?" one of the men asked.

"You have your Saturdays off. You are doing a fine work. Why don't you stay?"

Dan prayed about it. For some time he had had a great desire to become a minister. He'd been praying that the way would be opened for him. Could this discharge be the Lord's way of leading him? Dan decided to leave the Air Force. He'd go home and visit his father. This time it would be a joyous occasion.

Dan went home with all his good intentions and saying to himself, "This time I can make it." When he arrived at the hometown, there were his father and his old companions standing on the station platform. His companions urged him to spend just a little time with them, and Dan in his own strength could not withstand their pressure. Now he came to realize that he was an alcoholic. Liquor he could not resist. For the third time Dan watched his father leave the depot alone, stooped and weary, while he went with his friends.

The next day he felt utterly helpless and hopeless again. "It's no use!" he cried. "I can't stand firm. I might as well throw everything overboard." That evening he walked out of his father's house, looked up at the stars and said, "God, please leave me alone. I'm not going to make it to heaven. There's no use working myself to death and still not make it. I know I am going to be lost. I might as well have a good time while I'm here." He paused and then added, "Get out of my life and leave me alone."

He bade his father good-bye.

"I'll keep praying for you, Son," Father said, his voice weak with emotion.

Dan went to Oklahoma where his brother Don now lived. Don was a successful chiropractor in Woodward. The two brothers were glad to see each other after the years of separation. Don helped Dan find a job. He helped him find a place to stay. But soon Dan began to drink and carouse. Since he had ordered God from his life, things went from bad to worse. He became involved in fights and brawls all over town.

For two-and-a-half years he lived in Woodward, fully realizing that he was a failure. Although occasionally he attended the little Seventh-day Adventist church in Woodward, he had no desire now to go to school or become a minister. He told himself over and over that he had no need nor use for God. He could get along!

7

A Miraculous Birth

Dan worked in a large store in the paint and wallpaper department. During the day he wore a simulated smile on his face. At night he hurried home to his bottle. There was no peace or joy in his heart.

One day two women came into the store. Dan offered to help the younger woman who wanted some wallpaper and some paint. He learned that she was a Mrs. Bunch. She and her husband and son lived on a farm not far from town and they owned a choice herd of cattle. He learned that the older woman with her was her mother-in-law.

Dan felt a little uncomfortable as he became aware that the younger woman was scrutinizing him while he mixed the paint she wanted.

Suddenly she asked, "Haven't I seen you in church?"

"What church?" Dan laughed.

"The Seventh-day Adventist church," she replied.

Dan shook his head. "No, my work keeps me busy until noon, so it couldn't have been me. I'm not a churchgoer."

After a few more minutes had passed, she probed, "Are you sure you weren't visiting our church? You came late and left early?"

"Oh," Dan felt his face flush. "Yes, I guess I did visit that church." Then he told the two women that his parents had joined the Seventh-day Adventist Church years ago, and that from time to time he had attended.

Soon after the two women left the store, Dan was surprised to see the younger woman return with a man she introduced as her husband, Melvin. Dan felt warmed by their friendliness. "Why, they seemed genuinely interested in me," he said to himself as they left the store.

About an hour later, Dan was startled to hear Melvin's voice. He turned from where he was sitting at a desk and then stood up. Melvin, with a smile on his face was coming toward him.

"Say, we'd like to have you come to our home for dinner," he invited.

Dan stepped back, a little embarrassed. He hadn't been invited to anyone's home in Woodward. Even Don didn't seem anxious to have him around now. "Thanks," he hesitated, "I—I'd like to do that, but—but I have an appointment this evening. Another time, maybe."

Melvin shook his hand and said. "Fine. Another time then," and turned to leave.

Once more Dan went about his work in the store. He was waiting on a customer when out of the corner of his eye he saw Marilyn and Melvin Bunch coming toward him. They waited until he had finished with the customer then Marilyn said with a smile, "We were just thinking how nice it would be if you would come to camp meeting next Sabbath. We could have dinner together. We'd love to have you."

"Camp meeting? Where is the camp meeting?" Dan asked as he laughed nervously.

"In Oklahoma City," Melvin answered.

"That's impossible," Dan felt relieved but tried to sound disappointed. "I couldn't make it. That's one hundred and fifty miles away, and the store is open until noon on Saturdays."

He noticed the look that passed between the Bunches. Then Marilyn said, "What about being there for the evening meal?"

"Why should these people take such an interest in me?" he thought. It took him a little off guard. Before he had time to think it through, he had accepted the invitation to be at the camp meeting and to eat the evening meal with them on Saturday.

Melvin wrote their name and the address of the campground on a slip of paper and handed it to Dan. "We'll see you next Sabbath," he said, giving Dan's arm a light touch.

There were customers waiting, and Dan now hurried to serve them. He had little time the rest of the day to think about the strange meeting with the Bunches. But when evening came, he thought about it. It had seemed so casual at first, but then an invitation to dinner and then to camp meeting. They acted as if he were an old friend. "Huh," Dan decided, "I guess they are going to try to convert me. I should have seen through that. Now why did I promise to go to Oklahoma City?"

Before the next day, Dan had made up his mind that he didn't want to become involved. He would not go to Oklahoma City, at least he would not go to the campgrounds.

A day or two later Dan recognized the older Mrs. Bunch in the store. He would ask her to give his regrets to Melvin and Marilyn. "Will you please tell them my plans have changed. I'll not be able to keep my date with them on the campgrounds."

"I'll see that they get the message," Mrs. Bunch replied.

Dan tried to forget the whole incident. Really, there was no reason why he should think about this couple that had been so friendly and kind to him. He had decided not to meet them at the campground. And that was that.

On Saturday morning Dan went to work as usual. He hurried home at noon to shower, rest a bit, have something to eat, and then spend the long evening in a bar.

All the while he showered he thought of the Bunches. When he stretched out on the bed for a rest, he thought of them. He wondered if they would be disappointed. Well, why should it bother him? He shrugged. Of course, there'd be an empty plate at the table. He couldn't get the picture of that empty plate to go away.

Then he had an idea. He would go to Oklahoma City. He had a buddy there. His buddy always had something to do on a Saturday night. He'd go to the campgrounds first. No doubt there would be so many people there that he'd never be able to find the Bunches. He'd leave a note letting them know he had been there.

"Now, where did I put that piece of paper Melvin Bunch gave me with the address of the campgrounds on it?" Dan began to search his pockets. Well, if he couldn't find the address— Then he decided he could call the church pastor and get the address.

The pastor answered the telephone when Dan called. He gave the address and the directions to the campgrounds. Then he added, "It is a good thing you called when you did. I had left for the campgrounds, but remembered something I had left at the house so I returned for it and was just leaving as the phone rang."

Dan thanked the pastor and left the house. He started down the highway with the resolve to find the campgrounds, leave a note for the Bunches, and then call his buddy and make plans with him for an evening on the town. He whistled as he drove along. He'd never be so foolish again as to agree to go where there was a religious meeting going on!

In about three hours Dan reached the turn in the road that lead to the campgrounds. He hadn't gone far when he noticed a slight incline and there at the top stood a metal pavillion.

"That's some size!" Dan exclaimed as he found a place to park the car off the highway. And then he saw the tents—a sea of tents. "If only Mother could have seen this," he said. "I don't suppose Mother even knew about camp meetings. She never talked about one." And there was the pavillion right ahead of him now and a sign above it that said: "Jesus Is Coming Soon."

He stopped and stared. He blinked and shook his head. There were people coming out of the pavillion. People everywhere. And as he stopped and looked around in amazement someone slapped him on the shoulder. He turned quickly.

"We just knew you'd come," Melvin Bunch said with a friendly grin. The afternoon meeting had just been dismissed. That's why there were so many people milling around right then.

Dan couldn't tell Melvin Bunch he didn't intend to stay. He

allowed himself to be taken to a section where there were tables set out under the trees. There Melvin introduced him to Miriam, Marilyn's sister, who had just returned from mission service in Ethiopia. He introduced him to the members of the Woodward Church who were eating with Miriam, Melvin, Marilyn, and their son Ron. That meal Dan enjoyed more than any he'd had in a long time. These people were so friendly. He'd not found friends like these since he'd left the little church in North Carolina near the Air base.

But as soon as the meal was over, Dan stood up and apologized for having to eat and run.

Little Ron Bunch, sitting next to him, slipped his small hand into Dan's. "We wanted you to stay for the evening meeting. Couldn't you please stay?"

Dan looked at his wristwatch. "Well, what time will the meeting be over?" he asked.

"Oh, by nine o'clock," he was told.

He hesitated. He didn't want to stay. But these folk had been so good to him. "Well, I suppose I could stay." Then he turned to Marilyn. "Don't expect me to take a stand at the meeting," he said.

Now why had he said that? He felt a little foolish about it.

Melvin urged Dan to sit with him while he recorded the service. They sat on the front row. Miriam, Marilyn, and Ron sat a few rows back. Dan looked around and watched the people filing in. In a short time the pavillion was packed. Then a long line of ministers marched in while hushed organ music filled the auditorium.

"How Mother would have enjoyed this!" kept running through Dan's mind. A couple stepped onto the platform and sang "In the Garden." That was one of his mother's favorites. Then two young men sang "The Old Rugged Cross."

When the evangelist stepped up to the podium, Dan leaned back in his seat. He was eager but somewhat apprehensive about listening. The evangelist certainly had poise. He opened the Bible and began to speak. Dan leaned forward now and drank in the words telling of the love of our heavenly Father for sinners and how Christ died for them.

"He's talking to me," Dan thought. "I am a sinner. I made the decision to get Christ out of my life. I decided against heaven." But as he listened to the sermon, for the first time in his life he began to understand what salvation really means. He realized why Christ had died for sinners.

"That means me!" Dan said over and over in his heart. Then he decided, "If He really loves me so much, I want to be saved."

Soon the evangelist was making an altar call. "If Christ is speaking to your heart tonight, do not turn away."

Not a person stood up. It was so quiet that Dan could hear his heart thumping. The evangelist seemed to be talking only to him. He changed position in his seat. He tried to get away, but there was the call again. Well, he'd tried before. He'd been a failure. It wasn't right to make a commitment again that he couldn't keep.

"Of course, in your own strength you can do nothing. You are doomed to be a failure," Dan heard the evangelist say. "But God is always ready and eager to hear the faintest cry for help. Do not put off the invitation," the man spoke softly and earnestly. "It may be forever too late!"

"Too late! Too late!" the words repeated themselves in Dan's mind. Dan sat, gripping his chair. Now he loosened his hold. "Too late!" He squirmed in his seat and fastened his grip once more.

"How many of you would be ready, if you had a wreck that cost your life on the way home?"

Dan thought about his buddy and the party he planned to attend later. He knew that after the party when he drove home he would be under the influence of liquor. He always drove too fast when he'd been drinking. He'd been saved at least three times from fatal injuries. Of his twelve old high-school buddies, eleven had been killed in car accidents. All these things flashed through his mind. He'd been in twenty-two car accidents—in eight of them the cars had been totaled. He'd been shot at three times, struck over the head so many times he couldn't count them all. He'd had his nose broken four times, and he'd even been stabbed.

"Now, why has my life been spared?" he asked himself. Then he thought, "God has been good to me. So many of my old buddies are gone." Something said to him "Why don't you surrender? Surrender all."

Dan let loose his grip on the chair and stood to his feet.

To his astonishment when he arose others stood too. Had they been waiting for him to take his stand? Now a great weight seemed to be lifted from his shoulders. He would probably lose his job, but he didn't care. The Lord had done so much for him, what he did in comparison was small. Nothing mattered but his decision to follow his Saviour. How he wished Mother could know of this. Dan knew he would never be the same.

That evening Dan stayed on the campgrounds talking with his new friends. He forgot about his planned partying. He forgot his cigarettes. He forgot about the liquor in his car. His newfound Saviour was all he wanted and needed.

That date in August, the last meeting of the Oklahoma City camp meeting in 1962, was the turning point in Dan's life. He'd never forget it!

8

Victory

Dan knew he had miraculously changed. His friends found a place for him to stay on the campgrounds that night. When morning came, he felt like a new man. Everything seemed so alive and beautiful. He knelt with the Bunches while they prayed asking God to be with him on his way home and thanking Him for his victory. With a fond farewell to Marilyn and Melvin and little Ron, Dan slipped behind the wheel of his car and headed for Woodward.

As he drove, he thought of all that had happened since he had arrived at camp meeting less than twenty-four hours before. Now on his way back to town, he reached over to turn on his car radio. Loud music boomed out. He turned the knob to another station. Western music was his favorite. He had always enjoyed sitting behind the wheel, smoking a cigarette, and listening to Western music. Suddenly he felt the need of a cigarette. He reached into his pocket. It was empty. Then he looked up at the visor on the windshield. There was his pack of cigarettes. Dan grabbed the wheel tightly and looked away from the temptation.

"I am not going to give in. I choose not to smoke. I won't smoke." He looked up at the pack of cigarettes on the visor. "You're there and I want you, but I don't want you," he said out loud.

His face felt flushed. Beads of perspiration covered his forehead. Then in desperation Dan cried out, "Lord, is this the way it's going to be? Don't let me fail again. Please, help me, Lord."

That evening the evangelist had made it quite clear that no matter what he had done he was pure and clean from that moment on. Dan believed he was forgiven. He remembered the words from the Bible, "Come now, and let us reason together, saith the Lord: though your sins be as scarlet, they shall be as white as snow; though they be red like crimson, they shall be as wool." And there was another text, "If any man be in Christ, he is a new creature." These texts Dan had learned when he was back in North Carolina in the Air Force days. He remembered them when the evangelist had used them last evening. Those texts had given him strength through hardships put on him before. Now he was under pressure. He wanted victory.

His foot pressed harder and harder on the accelerator. The car leaped forward. Those cigarettes on the visor kept beckoning him. "More than once I've thrown those dirty things away," Dan thought, "only whenever rough times came I got more. Now what?" Over and over he repeated aloud: "I choose not to smoke. I choose not to smoke." Finally the white line in the road looked like a long cigarette to him.

"This is just not going to work," he shouted, bringing his foot up from the accelerator, slowing the car. "God," he cried, "if You don't help me, I'll fail again. I have no strength of myself. Lord, help me."

Then as suddenly as the desire for a cigarette had come, that desire left. A great burden seemed to be lifted. Dan felt he would never again have a desire for another cigarette.

He drove on to Woodward with joy in his heart.

The next day Dan looked up from some paper work he was doing in the store to see Marilyn and Melvin Bunch coming toward him, their faces wreathed in smiles. Dan grasped Melvin's out-

stretched hand in both of his. "Am I glad to see you," he said, and
began to tell them his experience on the way home from the campgrounds.

"We will certainly pray for you, Dan." Melvin said. "You know,
we were praying for you Sabbath morning, praying that you
would come to camp meeting. The Lord answered that prayer.
What a God we serve! You call us at any time of day or night if
you need someone to talk to." Marilyn nodded agreement.

And Dan knew well that he would need all the help and prayers
he could get. Dan realized he would have a struggle to overcome
his craving for alcohol.

"Look at you, Dan," Marilyn said, "you must be at least six
feet tall and you're as thin as a rail. What you need is some good
food."

"I'm six feet two inches," Dan laughed. "I weigh only 130
pounds. I know I haven't been eating right. I am going to need
your prayers and your help. The old serpent isn't going to let me
give up my drinking habits easily." And Dan poured out his problem to his friends.

Many times in the nights that followed the temptation did become so strong to have a drink, just one drink, just one sip,
that Dan felt he could bear no more. Then he'd get up, get in his
car, and drive over to the Bunches. This happened time after
time. The time of day or night seemed to make no difference to
his friends. They were always willing to help and to pray for and
with him.

"Dan," Melvin said one evening when Dan called, "you must
claim a promise found in Matthew 7:7. The promise is that if you
ask you will receive." Then he went on, "Dan, do you believe that
God gave you the victory over cigarettes?"

"Certainly."

"Then do you believe He can give you the victory over liquor?"

Dan hesitated. "Well—yes," he answered slowly.

"Do you really believe that God can give you the victory?"
Melvin repeated.

Once more he hesitated. Then he answered, "Yes, yes, I do."

"Then let's pray for victory again," Melvin suggested. And Melvin and Dan prayed, claiming the promise.

The next night the urge to drink came upon Dan again. He suffered and battled alone until he could stand it no longer. He got out of bed and dropped to his knees. "Lord, I can't wake those dear friends anymore. You must help me. I feel that I will break under the pressure. You gave me the victory over cigarettes. I can't do anything in my own strength. Lord, help me." For a few moments Dan stayed on his knees. Then he got into bed and fell asleep.

The next morning he awoke feeling refreshed and clearheaded. He felt a joy and an exhilaration he'd never felt before. He whistled as he dressed. Then he hurried over to the Bunch farm to tell his friends the wonderful news.

Little Ron came running from the house when Dan entered the yard. "Uncle Dan, would you like to go on a picnic with us?" he asked looking up into Dan's face.

"Sure, I'd like to go on a picnic with my little buddy," Dan answered. "How about me bringing some roast chicken?" he asked Marilyn as she stood holding the door open for him and little Ron.

Dan didn't wait for an answer but began telling the wonderful experience of his victory over drink.

"Wonderful!" Melvin exclaimed, slapping Dan on the back. "Always remember that 'with God all things are possible.' Now, about the picnic."

"I'll bring a roasted chicken," Dan offered again.

"It's nice of you to offer to bring something," Marilyn said, "but, Dan, we don't really need the chicken. You see, we are vegetarians."

Dan looked from Marilyn to Melvin. "Vegetarians?"

"Vegetarians do not use meat," Melvin began to explain.

"But in the Bible there is a chapter that gives us a list of meats that are fit for food," Dan said, a perplexed look on his face. "It also mentions swine's flesh, frogs, etc., that are not clean meats. But what's wrong with beef, chicken, or fish?"

Then Melvin explained that God's original plan for man's diet as recorded in Genesis was fruit, grains, and nuts. "Not until after the Flood," he said, "did God permit flesh foods to be used for food. There was no vegetation then, so God gave Noah and his family permission to use flesh foods. But if you read those chapters in Genesis that tell about the life-span of men before and after the Flood, you'll note that when they began to eat meat, the life-span was shortened."

"I never thought about that." Dan stared at Melvin.

"You know," Marilyn spoke up, "today there is so much cancer and other diseases among animals that we certainly can't keep ourselves physically fit, or keep our bodies, the temple of the living God, in a healthy state if we put diseased things into them. God has supplied us with an abundance of natural food. Why should we resort to diseased meat or secondhand food?"

"You know," Dan said, "I agree with you. No more meat for me. Now, when do we have that picnic?"

After the picnic Marilyn gave Dan six cans of vegetarian chicken. The next day he opened one of the cans. "Looks like chicken breast to me," he said to himself. He whistled as he fried all the pieces and sat down to watch TV as he ate. Soon he opened another can and after frying those pieces of vegetarian chicken he ate them. That evening when he stretched out on his bed he glanced over at six empty cans on the counter. "Surely I didn't eat all that vegetarian chicken!" He shook his head. "It sure was good!"

When he met Melvin and Marilyn again and she asked how he liked the chicken, his eyes twinkled as he told her, "I ate all six cans the first day, that's how much I liked it. Now what do you think of me?"

Marilyn laughed. "Well, I think you might gain a little weight, and that won't hurt you."

"No, I guess it won't. I'm going to need every ounce of strength and help I can get," he answered solemnly. "My employer is not happy about me wanting Saturdays off. But I'm determined to stand for what is right."

"Well, the Lord has promised that He will provide," Marilyn replied. "Trust Him, Dan. And be assured we will be praying for you too."

Before the next Sabbath came, Dan had been told to look elsewhere for work. When he told his story to his Christian friends, they suggested "Why don't you go into the colporteur ministry, Dan? Get in touch with the Oklahoma Conference publishing director. You'd enjoy the colporteur work, and what an opportunity it would afford you to tell others of your newfound faith."

Dan needed little urging. He wrote the publishing director immediately and shortly after received a visit from him. Dan poured out his story. He told of his recent conversion, his love for God and his desire to help others.

"Well," the publishing director said after listening to Dan's story, "I am sure the colporteur ministry is the place for you. There's going to be a colporteur institute held very soon. Dan, you must plan to be there."

"I will," Dan promised.

And in a few short weeks Dan found himself going from home to home telling the good news of the love of God and of a soon-coming Saviour. He worked hard and met with much success in selling and delivering books in the Woodward area. He was not simply satisfied to take orders, but he told everyone of what the Lord had done for him.

One day Dan stopped to visit Marilyn and Melvin after his day's work. "Dan, I've been doing a lot of thinking about you lately," Marilyn said. "I think you should go back to school. You know, my mother lives near Pacific Union College. That's in California. She has taken a lot of young people into her heart and home. Why don't you plan to attend P.U.C. next school year?"

"Back to school!" Dan thought it over.

At last he decided he would go to school. But California and Pacific Union College were out west. He settled on Madison College in Tennessee, and the next school year found him there. He arrived on the campus on a Friday afternoon. The school, he learned, had just enjoyed a special spiritual emphasis week. That evening was to be the last meeting of the series. He went to chapel with the other young people and listened to their shared experiences.

"What a group to be among!" Dan thought to himself. Only a few months before he had attended a wonderful camp meeting—the greatest thing he had ever done in his life. Now, here he was with a group of young people who seemed glowing with their love for God, the God that he too had learned to love. Dan could sit still no longer. He got to his feet: "I thank God I am here this evening," he began. "I'd like to share in this wonderful service with you. You will never know what it means to me to be here." Dan paused. Then he went on slowly, "Friends, only a few months ago I was living a life of sin. Everything looked as black as night then. But when Jesus Christ found me, He changed my life completely and it became as bright as day. What a hope and peace I now have!"

Dan felt the quietness in the room. He looked around at the students who all seemed to be looking at him with a sort of radiant glow. He went on to tell them how he had longed to be a Christian. How he had tried in his own strength and failed. But then he had let the Lord have full control of his life. He knew his sins had been forgiven, and he was happy to have final victory over those sins and to start a new life.

For a moment after Dan sat down there was complete silence. Then an audible sound of sighs escaping and "Amens" from various places in the room.

After the service Dick Forrester, the dean of men, stepped up to Dan and shook his hand. "I'm sure God has a place for you in His work," the dean said, placing his hand on Dan's arm. Then he introduced his wife, Dottie.

"Welcome to Madison." Dottie Forrester smiled and shook Dan's hand.

Dan walked to his room with a happy heart. Here he was at a Christian college. He would learn more of the Bible and God's will for him. This Sabbath would be one of the highlights in Dan's life. "If only Mother could share these moments with me," he thought.

Early Sunday morning Dan went to register. He was surprised to find several persons ahead of him. He was impressed with their friendliness.

When at last his turn came to register and the registrar asked in what field he wished to major Dan spoke up, "Bible." The registrar took off his glasses and looked up at Dan. "Everyone takes Bible courses. Now what is your field? In what do you wish to major?"

"Bible. I want to major in Bible," Dan repeated, a little perplexed.

"Yes, but, do you wish to take theology, Bible instructor's course—or what is your—your special interest so far as a lifework is concerned?"

"I just want to study the Bible," Dan replied.

"Well, young man, perhaps you should try another school. We do teach Bible as a regular part of our curriculum, but there are other colleges that specialize in Bible-related subjects."

Dan turned away. He couldn't speak. Here he had come to study the Bible. They were sending him away. He got out of the large student-filled room in a hurry, with head down he wandered along the street, noticing nothing.

Suddenly a clap on the shoulder and the words, "Friend, it's good to see you," made him look up. There stood the dean, Dick Forrester.

"I came all the way here to study Bible," Dan blurted out. "They think I should go elsewhere!"

"Dan, don't let the devil discourage you," Dick Forrester said. "Come on, let's see what we can do. I know the Lord has a place for you in His work. You can get started right here. I have a friend who knows more about the Bible than most, and he'll be more than glad to teach you. Let's visit this man. Pastor Tindall is a real man of God."

At these words Dan felt cheered. His trip to Tennessee had not been in vain. And Pastor Tindall proved to be the help that Dan needed. They spent hours together studying God's Word.

"Danny," Pastor Tindall said one day when they had been studying together, "The Lord has called you to be an evangelist. You must go to one of our schools where they prepare young evangelists for their special work."

9

A New Note

"The Lord has called you to be an evangelist!" the words kept ringing in Dan's mind. He remembered how as a boy when Mother took him to church he had admired the ministers and their knowledge of the Bible. He remembered many times he had played he was an evangelist, swaying thousands of listeners. Now he knew he wanted to be an evangelist for the Lord, bringing many to a knowledge of God's love and His plan for mankind.

Dan's mind was occupied with these thoughts one Friday afternoon as he drove by the post office. There at the curb stood Dick Forrester's wife Dottie and a girl in a student nurse uniform.

Dan pulled up beside them. "May I offer you ladies a ride home?" he asked.

"Oh, thank you," Dottie answered with a smile. "This is Dick's sister Kay," she said, letting the young student nurse get in first.

The ladies chatted as Dan drove to the dormitory where the Forresters lived. Dan stopped the car and hurried around to help Dottie out. "I'll get out here too," Kay said. "I just live down the street and around the corner in Senior Hall."

"Oh, I'll be glad to take you there," Dan said, shutting the door and going around to the driver's side. "Just tell me where to turn," he said, driving on down the road.

"Right here! Right here," Kay said, pointing to the dormitory at the corner as Dan started to make the turn.

"Oh," he laughed. "I see I have much to learn about college life. You know I thought Senior Hall was a Senior Citizen's home."

Kay's laugh sounded like silver bells, Dan thought, as he helped her from the car. He couldn't help noticing the color of her eyes. The deepest blue he had ever seen.

"Thanks, Dan," she said. "I'm glad to finally meet you."

"What do you mean by 'finally'?" Dan queried.

"I heard your testimony on a Friday night not long ago. Dick and Dottie have spoken of you often since then."

Before Dan realized it he was sharing his experience of conversion and his plans for the future with this girl who in turn told him of her desires to witness to others of God's love.

"Oh, I must go in!" Kay suddenly exclaimed, looking at her wristwatch. "It's Friday, and it's getting late." She hurried up the dormitory steps and went in, leaving Dan standing on the walk staring after her.

Dan went to his car. He drove slowly to his room. "Maybe she would like to have dinner with me," he mused. He'd call her when he got home. But the girl that answered the phone to his call told him that Kay had gone for a walk. "Call back later," she suggested.

Dan called several times but with no luck.

At last he went to the college cafeteria alone. There was Kay sitting at the end of a table. Dan sauntered up behind her, bent down and spoke softly, "I tried to catch you earlier to ask you to have dinner with me." He looked around at the full table.

"Ask again sometime," she replied.

Was she a little flustered? Dan wondered as he sat down with his tray at another table. Well, he would ask her again. In fact, he planned to ask her to go with him several times.

Several weeks later Dan and a young couple planned to go to a little church in Alabama. Dan decided to ask Kay if she would go along.

"Of course! I'd love to go." Kay thanked Dan for the invitation.

Dan felt like shouting from the housetop. Kay was going to be his companion for the day! She was the nicest girl he had ever met. And they had so many things in common. Probably most in common was their love of Christ and their desire to tell others of that love.

On the way to the little church, converted from a sawmill, the two couples talked about God's wonderful Sabbath day. They shared Bible promises and sang as they journeyed.

The associate pastor spoke at the church service and then asked Kay if she would sing the closing song for them. Dan sat spellbound as her lovely voice floated out over the congregation.

That day Dan realized that Kay meant more to him than just a friend. He wondered how she felt toward him. He watched every expression on Kay's face as one of the church members, a little old lady, told them of how the church had started in that area. Her husband had not been an Adventist, she said. They had come to Alabama when her doctor had said that she had only six months at best to live. She had decided that during those six months she would tell as many souls as possible about the Lord. She had begun giving Bible studies as soon as they came to Alabama. And wonder of wonders, her heart grew stronger and within six months she was completely well. Not only did she receive a blessing as she worked for the Lord, but her husband was converted in that time as well.

"Just think, only six months to live," Kay said, her face glowing, "and in that time you raised up not only a nucleus for a church, but converted your husband and regained your own strength. All because of your dedication to God!"

"Ah, yes," Dan said. "I like the thought expressed in *The Desire of Ages* which says, 'There is no limit to the usefulness of one who, by putting self aside, makes room for the working of the Holy Spirit upon his heart.'"

"True, very true," Kay responded, looking up into Dan's eyes.

Kay and Dan said little on the drive back to Madison. The day had been full. Each seemed to be immersed in thought. Dan felt

a joy and peace he had rarely felt before. He let Kay off at the
dormitory after letting the other couple off first. For a moment
their hands touched as Dan said, "Good-night, Kay. This has been
a Sabbath day to remember."

Kay nodded and ran quickly up the steps into the dorm.

Christmas Day dawned. A silence covered the campus as the
snow fell softly but swiftly in large flakes, covering the ground.
Soon the silence was broken by the happy laughter and singing of
young people as they emerged from dormitories, some going
here and some there. Dan and Kay and several other students
planned to drive to Nashville to share yuletide joy with prisoners there. The group sang to the prisoners and Dan talked to
them. He well understood their feelings. He told of his joy in his
new life. Then Kay sang, "I would love to tell you what I think of
Jesus since I've found in Him a friend so strong and true; I would
tell you how He changed my life completely; He did something
that no other one could do."

Dan felt his throat grow tight. As Kay's voice filled the cold
prison chapel, every word seemed to have real meaning to her as
she sang. Dan wiped away a tear that moistened his cheek. Then
he looked around at the others in the room. There were few dry
eyes.

"What a wonderful witness she is!" Dan thought. "What a
wonderful girl!"

He had to leave Kay and the group at the college cafeteria after
returning from Nashville. He had been invited to have dinner
that day with a village family. How he wished he and Kay could
have Christmas dinner together! He'd return to her as soon as
possible, he decided as he let her off and went his way.

When he returned to the dormitory later in the afternoon, he
found Kay in the parlor with a group of girls. They were around
the piano and singing. Dan picked Kay out immediately. And as if
his eyes had beckoned her, she turned and smiled.

"I want to talk to you, Kay," he made the motion with his lips.

Kay left the group. She ran to her room for her coat and then
she and Dan started walking up the road from the dormitories
that had been dubbed the "King's Highway." Dan touched Kay's
elbow and steered her to a quiet place. "Kay," he said, "I have

been strongly attracted to your beautiful Christian character. Everything has been more meaningful in my life since I've met you. I must know, Kay, how do you feel toward me?"

Kay blushed. For a moment she looked down at the white snow covering the ground. Then, without looking up, she said, "Dan, I—I enjoy being with you. We seem to have the same vision." Then she looked into his eyes, "I can see that your heart is as full of love for the Lord as mine. I—I—"

"That's wonderful! That's all I need to know," Dan said, taking her hands in his. "This is the way I feel toward you too. We won't rush anything now. Let's let the Lord lead us."

Kay nodded, but he saw her eyes fill with tears, and somehow Dan knew those tears were tears of joy. "In June you'll graduate from nurse's training. In the meantime let's share every missionary project. Let's determine that in these months to come we'll witness for Christ at every opportunity," he added.

In the days that followed, Dan spent every moment possible with Kay when she was off duty. She told him how she had always dreamed of being a nurse, but it had seemed an impossible dream. The administration of Pine Forest Academy, where she had graduated, had decided to send her to Madison to take the nurse's training course, with the understanding that she return to the school as school nurse.

He told her about his mother, about his experiences in the Air Force and his several conversion experiences. He told her about his friends, the Bunches, in Oklahoma and the camp meeting he had attended where he had decided to make the real change in his life. He told her about the victories he had gained and his determination to be an evangelist someday.

Just before graduation Kay told Dan that she planned to go to California with Dottie and Dick that summer to visit Mother Forrester and other relatives.

"I'm glad for you," Dan said. "But, do you have any idea how much I shall miss our visits?"

Kay smiled up at him. "We've really had some wonderful experiences together, haven't we?" she said.

When Kay marched down the aisle in her cap and gown at graduation, Dan knew she was the most beautiful girl in her class.

Right after the ceremonies Dan suggested they go for a short ride together.

Kay got into his car. Dan drove to the lake nearby and parked. They had driven to the lake in complete silence. They had learned that silences between them were full of meaning. Dan helped Kay from the car, and they strolled by the lakeside. There was no need yet to talk. Then Dan stopped. He stepped in front of Kay and his arms went around her. "Kay," he whispered. "Kay, will you be my wife? Will you share your life with me?" Dan's heart pounded wildly as he waited for an answer.

Kay's head rested on his chest. Could she feel the wild beating?

He bent his head to hear her words. He couldn't be sure. "What did—what did you say, Kay?"

Then she lifted her head. He looked into her eyes. He heard the words, soft, but clear, "Yes, Dan, I want to share your life."

His lips found hers in that first kiss of promise.

And now with their arms about each other they walked down to the place where a boat was tied. Dan helped Kay into the boat. Kay let her fingers trail in the water while Dan rowed. Then Kay repeated some of her favorite psalms.

"Kay, will you do something for me?" Dan asked.

"You know I will," she smiled.

"Sing for me the song you sang at the Nashville jail on Christmas Day."

And Kay sang. "I would love to tell you what I think of Jesus."

All too soon Dan said, "I guess it is time for us to go back, sweetheart. I'll miss you so much this summer when you are in California. But, I thank God for your love and your desire to work for Him. You'll be going back to work at Pine Forest Academy, and we'll meet there."

10

Sorely Tempted

The day after watching Kay drive off to California with her brother Dick and sister-in-law Dottie, Dan decided to visit his father back in New Mexico. Dan wanted to tell his father all about the miracles the Lord had performed in his life. He wanted to tell him about the wonderful girl who had promised to share his life.

What a happy reunion Dan had with his father this time. During his stay he became acquainted with Kenneth Cox, an evangelist in that area. Dan and Pastor Cox spent much time together studying and sharing their faith. Pastor Cox was enthusiastic about self-supporting work, and within a few weeks Dan had caught a vision of a large work he and Kay could start around Pine Forest, where they planned to live after their marriage at Christmas.

At last the letter arrived in New Mexico that Dan had been waiting for. The letter postmarked in California. The letter from his own sweet Kay! He tore it open eagerly and began to read. But as he read, the smile left his face. "What does this mean?" he asked aloud. "What—what has happened? He reread the words, "I think it would be best if we were to be just friends at first when we meet again at Pine Forest. We can enlarge our friendship from there."

The sunshine of the day seemed to be completely hidden by dark, foreboding clouds of doubt and fear. "She has broken her promise. Why?" Dan sank into a chair and put his head down in his hands. "If I could only talk to her. But I don't even know where to telephone her."

It was only through study and prayer that Dan managed to get through the several days ahead. When his father mentioned a trip to visit his grandmother in nearby Clovis, Dan decided to go along. It would be good to see his cousin Joe whom he had not seen in years and his uncle. He remembered the summer his three uncles had taught him how to fight.

Joe and his dad, Dan remembered, had never seemed to get along. Dan wondered if things were better now? The uncle owned his own bar. Dan and Joe had run in and out of it at leisure all the summer he had spent with Grandma while Mother had gone to summer school. Yes, it had been a long time since he had seen Joe and Joe's dad.

Upon meeting, Joe suggested they take a ride over to his father's bar. Dan was anxious to see his uncle, but somewhat reluctant to go into the bar. When they reached the bar, another cousin came up to greet them and invited Dan and Joe to the counter for a drink.

"Excuse me," Dan said, "I'm going to the men's room. You two go find a place." He turned to go to the men's room. He felt very uncomfortable in the bar. "If I stay here in the men's room long enough," he thought, "they'll finish their drink and Joe and I can get out of here."

But when Dan walked out he saw his cousins at the bar with an empty glass at each of three places.

"Come on, Dan, have a drink on me," Joe urged.

"No, Joe, I don't drink anymore," Dan said.

"Aw, come on. One glass isn't going to hurt you," the other cousin said.

Dan shook his head.

"One drink and we'll go," Joe urged.

"Well," Dan began to reason. "One drink and we can get out of here. One drink won't hurt me."

Dan drank the one glass, then another and another.

When he and Joe finally staggered out of the bar Dan's mind was clouded. It was then that Joe suggested they drive to Alaska. "We can sure make money fast there," he urged. "Besides I want to get away from home."

"Sure! Why not?" the slurred words came from Dan's mouth.

Once more Joe got behind the wheel and started to drive. Dan slumped down into a sort of drunken stupor. On and on they drove. Darkness came and still Joe drove on. Finally they reached Los Angeles, their money almost gone. Dan now fully aware of what had happened felt deep remorse for his actions. But what could he do? How could he undo what had already been done. Hopelessness seemed to overwhelm him. They traveled on to San Francisco and beyond Oakland. Somehow they turned off the freeway onto a little less traveled highway. By now they were unkempt and very weary.

"Why, this is the Napa-Calistoga Highway," Dan exclaimed, reading a sign. "I wonder if this takes us through Saint Helena?"

"It's a few miles ahead," Joe remarked. "I saw a sign not far back. Why, you know anyone in Saint Helena?"

"Yes, and no. I have some friends in Oklahoma, Marilyn and Melvin Bunch. Marilyn's mother lives out here, and we should look her up."

"What's her name?" Joe asked.

Dan scratched his head. "Now isn't that something. I haven't the faintest idea. I never asked Marilyn what her maiden name was."

"Well, here we are in the Saint Helena city limits," Joe said. "Now what?"

"There's a college around here, Pacific Union College," Dan commented. "Let's see if we can find it. If we find the college, maybe we can locate Marilyn's mother."

The two drove through the main street of Saint Helena. Dan, still feeling wretched about his yielding to temptation had been spending much time as they traveled, talking silently to His heavenly Father, asking for forgiveness and strength. Now after praying again, he looked up and there was the sign, PACIFIC UNION COLLEGE.

He almost wrenched the wheel from Joe. "There! There! that's the road. Turn here."

They followed the signs until they came to the college on top of Howell Mountain. Since they did not know Marilyn Bunch's maiden name, they were at a loss for whom to ask. But Dan tried to explain a little about the family to several of the people they met. At last, tired and discouraged, the boys drove back to Saint Helena. They parked the car near the bus depot, where they slept that night.

When daylight came, the two unkempt cousins counted their cash. They didn't have enough money between them to buy a breakfast. They'd have to find some work and work for a while to get money for food and gas.

Joe started out to look for odd jobs. Dan went into the bus depot and spoke to a lady at the desk there. "Do you know a lady who lives near Pacific Union College and who takes care of elderly people and also keeps students in her home?"

"Why, yes, you must mean Mrs. Moore of Rose Haven. Let me give you her telephone number."

Dan thanked the lady for her help. He stepped into the phone booth and dialed the number he had been given.

A male voice answered the phone, but then a familiar voice spoke. Dan's heart did a somersault. "Marilyn? Marilyn Bunch?" he queried.

"Who is this?" the party at the other end asked.

"It's Dan. Dan Collins, remember me?"

"Dan, where are you?" Marilyn asked. "You know we've just been having a family reunion here and the last one of the boys was just about to leave when the phone rang. Miriam is here too. Now, where are you and what are you doing there?"

Dan told her the story.

"Wait right there, Dan. We'll come and get you," Marilyn said.

Twenty minutes later Dan sat in the front room at Rose Haven with Marilyn and her mother.

"Marilyn has told me the whole story," Mother Moore said

softly. "How I praise God for bringing you to us."

Dan sat with his head bowed. "What hurts me most is that I have let my Lord down."

"Thank God, Dan, the Lord is willing to forgive and forget. Remember He has promised that 'if we confess our sins, he is faithful and just to forgive us . . . , and to cleanse us.' You believe that, don't you?" Mother Moore asked.

Dan nodded. "Yes, I believe. But I have failed Him so often." Dan looked up. "But, with God's help I will never let Him down that way again."

Miriam came into the room as they were talking. She reached out her hand to him. "Dan, it is so good to see you again. I've thought and prayed about you many times since meeting you, last year. How did you get here?"

Dan suddenly remembered his cousin Joe back in Saint Helena. He told Miriam about their sudden trip from Clovis, New Mexico, and about Joe's having started out to look for work that morning.

"You must bring him here," Mother Moore spoke up. "We'll be glad to have both of you. Miriam, why don't you and Dan drive back to Saint Helena and get Joe. Remember, Dan, this is your home as long as you wish," she added.

That evening Marilyn suggested that Joe and Dan call their parents. "They must be very concerned about you," she said. "I couldn't sleep a wink if my boys were away from home and I didn't know where," she added.

At last Joe agreed to call his mother, and Dan called his father who had gone back home. "We are in California with some Christian friends," Dan said. "Please don't worry about us now."

Dan turned to Mother Moore, "You will never know what your warm welcome has meant to both of us. You are like my mother. She was always ready to love and forgive and to help me."

"And you are my son, Dan. I believe in adoption," she smiled up at Dan. "We are all adopted sons and daughters of the Lord's family. I pray that I shall be a faithful mother to all my children both by birth and by adoption."

The next day since Marilyn and all the others who had been at the family reunion had left, Miriam took Dan and Joe sightseeing. She took them to the college and to Elmshaven.

"Oh, I think I'd like to come here and go to school," Joe said as he looked around the college campus.

"Without a doubt, I'll be back," Dan commented.

The boys decided to stay at Rose Haven over the Sabbath and then start for home on Sunday. Miriam had made a huge lunch for them to take with them. Mother Moore insisted that they fill the car with gas at a nearby filling station and use her credit card to do so.

Dan hesitated. Then he promised, "We'll pay you back as soon as possible."

Just then Mrs. Moore's cook at Rose Haven came along and offered Dan some money. "My son has just cashed a check for me and brought me this money. You need it right now, so I want you to use it."

The boys left Rose Haven dressed in clean clothes, with clear minds, and the funds to pay for their needed gas along the way. Waving and shouting good-byes they drove down the road and were soon out of sight of their new friends and Mother Moore.

Down the Napa-Calistoga Highway they drove. On either side the road were vineyards and the occasional winery. Suddenly Joe turned off the road and stopped at a wayside bar.

"What are you stopping here for?" Dan asked.

"For a drink. I'm parched," Joe replied. "Come on, let's have one."

Dan spoke firmly, "No, Joe, I'm not going in."

"Aw, come on. Just one," Joe insisted.

"No, sir. You go in if you want to," Dan said, "but when you return I'll not be here." He took out one of the ten dollar bills that the cook had given them before they left Rose Haven. Here's your part of the money. I refuse to go in."

Dan stepped out of the car as Joe made his way into the bar. A car stopped almost immediately and the driver asked, "You need a ride, young fellow?"

A few days later Dan reached his father's house in New Mexico. He paused at the gate to offer a silent prayer to his heavenly Father for His watchcare and guidance all the way to California and back.

11

His Father's Business

As Dan walked into the house, he thought of the several times that he had come home to his father and had greatly disappointed him. He wondered if Father would be able to forgive him this time. Could Father ever trust him again? He'd failed so miserably before.

But Dan knew, when Father Collins opened his arms to him, that even as his heavenly Father had forgiven him and loved him, so his earthly father loved him and forgave him. Dan opened up his heart to his father. He told him first of how the Lord had provided for him all the way. Then he told him the story of going into the bar with Joe. "That awful experience and getting drunk is like a nightmare," he said. "I thank God for people like dear Mother Moore of Rose Haven who took both me and Joe in, dirty, unkempt as we were, and loved us and cared for us." Then he added, "Now I must find a job. I want to go to school this year. I'd like to go to Pacific Union College."

"Son, your mother would be proud of you if she were here. I

know everything will turn out for the best. I guess I haven't said this very often to you, but I love you. I pray for you. And I know that as Paul the apostle said, 'All things work together for good to them that love God.' "

Dan began searching for a job. It wasn't what he wanted but the offer came to him to do trucking. He took it and with his first paycheck, he sent back the money that had been borrowed from the cook at Rose Haven in California. He wrote Mother Moore and those under her roof telling of his experience and joy in witnessing for his Saviour. He ended his letter by saying, "I hope to see you all soon, as I plan definitely on coming out to California and going to school at Pacific Union College this fall."

One day while at his job he met an old buddy of his. Mike and Dan had often visited bars together in the old days.

"Come on, Dan, let's have a drink," Mike urged.

Dan smiled, "Things are different now, buddy, I don't drink."

Mike laughed. "What's the matter? Have you gone religious?"

"You might say so," Dan answered. "I have Jesus Christ in my heart."

"You have what?" Mike laughed.

Dan told Mike how the Lord had led him and helped him overcome his old habits and had given him a joy he had never had before.

Mike stared at Dan. "You really mean it, buddy?' he asked.

Dan nodded then added, "Mike, will you do something for me?"

"Well, I—don't know—what is it?"

"Let me study the Bible with you. It's God's Book, Mike; and it's true. It has changed my life completely." Dan watched Mike as he seemed to be thinking over what he had said.

"Well—" Mike finally spoke up hesitatingly, "I—I guess it— it would be OK. Sure, you can study with me."

Dan clapped his friend on the shoulder. "Fine. Let's set a time right now."

It took some doing to get Mike pinned down to a time and place, but Dan stayed right with him until it had been settled. Then with a song in his heart Dan bade his friend good-bye and went on his way whistling.

On the appointed evening for the Bible study Dan set out early. "I'm going to give my first study!" he kept repeating over and over. But when he reached Mike's place, no one answered his knock on the door. Mike's place was in darkness. Dan realized that Mike had not meant to keep his promise.

A few days later the two met quite by accident. Dan sensed that Mike felt ill at ease. But Dan greeted his friend cheerily and then asked, "Say, did you forget about the Bible study?"

"I guess I did," Mike answered. "Look, Dan, I don't want anything to interfere with my way of life. Let's forget it."

"What are you afraid of, Mike?" Dan asked. "I just want you to know what the Good Book has done for me. That can't hurt you. How about it? Won't you let me come over and tell you about it?"

"OK! OK!" Mike agreed. "Let's make it the same time next week as we'd planned."

They parted. But the next week when Dan kept the appointment, Mike was not at home. The next week Dan went back, but Mike was still not there.

Dan turned from Mike's door with a determined step. He knew just where he'd find his old buddy. He walked down the street to the corner bar. There was a slight hesitation as he opened the door and then walked into the dimly lighted, smoke-filled room. "Father, go with me tonight and help me to save a soul," he prayed silently. Then he glanced over at the bar and saw Mike sitting there, a glass in his hand.

"Hello, friend," Dan said as he stepped up to Mike. "You let me down again. Tonight is the night we were going to have a Bible study."

"Yeah?" Mike turned on the bar stool. "I guess that's right. Well, give it to me right here," he slurred his words and pounded his fist on the bar.

"Right here?" It took Dan by surprise.

"Sh—shure, why not?"

Dan looked around. Several of the men in the room had stepped a little closer. They seemed partly amused.

"Go ahead," one of the men mumbled.

"All right," Dan agreed. "If that's what you wish, I'll just go out to my car and get my Bible." And he hurried out.

6—M.S.D.

"Oh, Father, give me the right words to speak," he prayed as he returned to the men who had gathered around the end of the bar.

Dan looked over his motley audience. Before he had time to begin, one of the men asked, "Say, how come you got all that religion? You used to be one of us."

Another spoke up, asking a question.

Dan had no time for a formal Bible study. He spent the time answering the questions the men threw up at him one after the other, until one of the men asked about the mark of the beast.

Suddenly the room was silent. Dan looked around the room. Now there was a question he couldn't answer.

"Yeah, tell us about the mark of the beast," another said.

Dan held up his hands for silence. "I am not able to answer that question for you," he said, "but I can have someone here in just a few minutes who can, if you want me to."

"Yeah!"

"Go ahead."

"We want to hear."

"Then excuse me for a few minutes," Dan said.

The men stepped aside, and Dan hurried from the barroom to an adjoining room where there was a pay telephone. Quickly he dialed the number of his friend, Pastor Cox.

"Pastor, can you come immediately to the bar down on the corner of Main and Elm? I have some folk there who want to know about the mark of the beast."

"But, Dan, I've already retired," the pastor's voice came over the phone.

"Pastor, I am in earnest. These men need to know now."

In a short time Pastor Cox arrived and entered the barroom where the men gathered around the pastor and Dan and listened to every word Pastor Cox said. They asked questions, and in his kind, gentle way, the pastor read the answers from the Bible. The pastor and Dan stayed with the men and talked until the bartender told them it was closing time.

"You'll talk to us some more, won't you?" several pleaded as Dan and the pastor left the men on the sidewalk outside the bar.

"We'll arrange a time with Mike," Dan assured the men.

But for several days Dan did not see Mike. "Is he trying to avoid me?" Dan wondered. He inquired around and was at last told that Mike had been in an accident and was hospitalized.

That evening, Dan visited his old buddy in the hospital.

"I'm glad you came to see me," Mike said from his hospital bed where he lay swathed in bandages. "If I ever get home again, I truly want you to study with me, Dan. I'm a sinner. I'm not ready to die." Tears flooded his eyes.

"Friend," Dan said, placing his hand on Mike's arm, "Christ came to save sinners. The Good Book says, 'Believe on the Lord Jesus Christ, and thou shalt be saved.' I'm going to have a word of prayer for you right now. The Lord can heal you if He sees fit. The Lord can forgive you at any time you ask Him, and He is ever waiting and willing. Let's just close our eyes while I pray."

There were tears streaming down Mike's face when Dan finished praying. "You'll come again, won't you?" he begged as Dan left.

Dan saw Mike regularly. And when Mike was at last told he could go home, true to his word he asked Dan to come and study the Bible with him.

Before long Dan saw Mike give his heart to the Lord. Mike gave up smoking and drinking and other bad habits, and Dan had the joy of seeing him baptized.

"You know," Dan said, "the Lord brought me right back into the bar where a short time before I had failed. Now I have been able with God's help to prove to the enemy that my God whom I serve is all-powerful and able to keep me from falling." Then he hastened to add, "This time, my only reason for going into a bar was to save a soul."

"And thank God for that," Mike nodded.

A few days later Pastor Cox told Dan of his plan to hold an evangelistic meeting in Raton, a town about eighty miles from Clayton where Dan lived with his father. "Dan," Pastor Cox said, "if you will help me in this effort, I'll pay you $100."

"Friend," Dan replied immediately, "it would be such a joy and privilege that I'd work without pay."

Up and down the streets of Raton Dan walked, leaving literature at every home. Then there was the setting up of the bubble tent that Pastor Cox had borrowed from the conference. Dan worked hard those days. At night his muscles often ached. But he could hardly wait for the opening evening. At each meeting he was to give a fifteen minute health talk. Dan studied and prayed much for himself and for the evangelistic meetings.

Raton was a Catholic town. Almost 90 percent of the population belonged to the Catholic faith. At the first meeting, the attendance was small. However, as the meetings progressed, more and more came until the place was filled.

"Dan," Pastor Cox said one day after reading his mail, "I have here a letter from the conference. They need this tent. I guess we'll have to wind up our meetings."

"We can't do that," Dan spoke up. "I'm sure we have a genuine interest here. We've put our hand to the plow, so to speak. Let's not turn back."

Pastor Cox gripped Dan's hand. "Spoken like a true soldier of Christ," he said.

That evening Pastor Cox asked the audience for a show of hands if they were interested in having the meetings continued. Dan could hardly contain his joy at seeing the response.

He and Pastor Cox found a building they were able to rent, and the meetings went on. At the end of the series thirty persons were baptized, and the nucleus of a Seventh-day Adventist church was established.

At the close of the series Dan determined he would never again work outside the organized work. "This has been such a blessed experience," he added.

"The Lord has called you to the ministry," Pastor Cox told his young assistant. "You must go to Pacific Union College and take theology."

Dan remembered the words of Pastor Tindall back in Tennessee, "Danny, the Lord has called you to be an evangelist." He also thought of his desire at the time of his conversion in the Air Force. He believed with all his heart that the Lord had a special work for him to do.

There was, however, a vacant spot in his heart. Often he thought of Kay. His love for her had never diminished. Why, oh why, had she written him as she had? He had never heard from her again.

Of course, he himself had not written. He had felt too crushed. He had thrown himself into his work with Pastor Cox, but there were times when he longed for the Christian girl with whom he wanted to share his life. Just to talk over the experiences in this series of meetings, just to talk over the goals they had established together. Was this not to be for him?

Dan kept repeating many of God's promises over and over. He believed that "all things work together for good" because he did love the Lord with all his heart. He determined to go back to school, come September, and to prepare himself further for the work of evangelism.

Late in September Dan returned to Rose Haven and Pacific Union College, and on registration day he was ready to register and prepare for that wonderful work that both Pastor Cox and Pastor Tindall had assured him should be his avocation.

Day after day and week after week he struggled now with his required lessons. His mind had not been trained to concentrate. It had been years since he had attended school.

"It is the devil trying to discourage me," he often said to Mother Moore as he poured over his assignments and found them harder and harder.

"Don't give up, Son. You'll make it," Mother Moore encouraged with her sweet smile.

But one day one of his instructors called him into the office. "Dan," he said, "you are not making it. Before you go any farther, I would advise you to consider another vocation. Really, Dan, you are not college material."

Dan sat stunned. What about evangelism? Why was he here? He had come for one thing, and that was to prepare for evangelism.

Slowly he left the instructor's office. Blindly he made his way down the road to Rose Haven. "They told me I'm not college material—that I should change my vocation!" The words burst from his lips as he came into the house and saw Mother Moore reading in her favorite corner of the room.

"Danny—" Mother Moore stood up and placed her hand up on Dan's shoulder— "Danny, what was it you said the other night? Remember? The old devil, you said, was trying to discourage you.

Don't let him. I have read the statement more than once, and I believe it, don't you? 'Not more surely is the place prepared for us in the heavenly mansions than is the special place designated on earth where we are to work for God.' There are many things you can do for God. Let's pray about it."

He and Mother Moore knelt, and both prayed for strength and guidance.

"You've done a fine work since you've been working after classes down at the Saint Helena Hospital, Danny," Mother Moore said as they rose from their knees. "You've had so many opportunities to talk to patients about their souls, as well as give them your best service. Now don't you give up, my boy," Mother Moore encouraged.

Dan gave up his classes at the college but kept up with his work at Saint Helena. While working there Dan met Mr. McFarland, who invited the young orderly to use his personal library at any time. Dan spent many hours after work studying and doing research in the McFarland library. He committed Bible text after text to memory. He would not give up his dream of entering evangelism. Neither could he forget the girl who had once promised to share that dream with him. Perhaps someday—

One Sabbath while driving home from church, Dan was stopped by a woman going in the opposite direction. Always a gentleman, Dan politely gave her directions. Something stirred within him as he talked to her. Her face seemed familiar. When he learned that she was Mrs. Forrester, his heart missed a beat.

"Are you by any chance the mother of Dick Forrester?" he asked, almost afraid to have her answer.

"Why, yes, I have a son named Dick," she said. "Do you know him?"

Dan ignored the question and rushed on. "Is Kay your daughter?"

Mrs. Forrester laughed. "Why, yes, Dick and Kay are my son and daughter."

Then Dan told Mrs. Forrester who he was and about his friendship with Dottie and Dick, and his admiration for Kay.

Mrs. Forrester smiled. "You know, Kay has talked about you. I really feel I know you. She hasn't said much about it lately, but

I'm sure she has a great admiration for you."

"Mrs. Forrester, won't you please come home with me to Sabbath dinner at Rose Haven? That's where I live right now. I want Mother Moore to meet you." And so Dan led the way to Rose Haven where he introduced Kay's mother.

What an experience! What could it all mean—meeting Kay's mother that Sabbath afternoon? "Some might call it chance, but I say the Lord is leading," Dan told his Rose Haven family at sundown worship that evening.

In the days that followed, Dan visited Kay's mother often. They became well acquainted, and Dan thrilled every time Mrs. Forrester told him she had another letter from Kay and shared it with him.

Christmas came that year with its memories. What memories! Just one year ago, Dan recalled, he and Kay had made the trip to the jail in Nashville. He remembered the song she had sung. It had been that evening that he had told Kay of his love for her. Only months later she had promised to share his love and his life. They had planned to be married this Christmas. How things had changed! They were miles and miles apart. He was not in school. He was not taking the courses that would prepare him for evangelism, his goal. What did God have in mind for him?

Once again it was spring. The campus of Pine Forest Academy in Tennessee was carpeted with green. Flowers bloomed in a profusion of colors. Birds had been building nests and singing their melodious bird songs for some weeks. Kay Forrester, the school nurse, found great joy in communing with her heavenly Father out in nature. She spent as much time as possible walking around the campus, in the nearby woods, and by the stream. Many times as she walked she thought of Dan Collins, the man who had asked her to be his wife. The man she had felt sure she could love and trust and share her joys and sorrows with for the rest of her life. What had happened to that wonderful relationship? Kay thought and prayed about it. What had gone wrong? Surely there had been a terrible misunderstanding. But what? If only she knew what to do.

One day, after returning from her walk, a friend met her with the news, "Kay, an old friend of yours is on the campus."

Kay, having been thinking of Dan, looked up startled. "Who?" she asked breathlessly.

"Why, Pastor Tindall, of course."

Kay could hardly keep a slight disappointment from her voice. "Oh!" was all she said. Of course it would be nice to see Pastor Tindall again, and she was more than happy to learn that he would be at her brother Dick's home that evening to dinner, and Dottie had invited her too.

"It is certainly nice that Dick and Dottie are here at Pine Forest too," Pastor Tindall said after greeting her that evening. "You know what I think would be nice?" He gave Kay a strange little smile and Kay noticed a special twinkle in his eye as he went on. "I wish Danny Boy were here."

Kay looked down at the floor. She hoped no one would see the longing look that must show in her eyes. Oh, there was nothing that she wished more than that at the moment too.

During the evening meal Pastor Tindall told about plans he was making to hold a series of meetings. Then he added, "I wish Dan could share my plans and help me with the meetings."

"Wouldn't that be great," Dick agreed.

Kay twisted the napkin in her hands in her lap. "Yes, that would be wonderful! It has been so long since we've seen him."

Later when Kay and Dottie were visiting in Kay's apartment, they began to talk about the possibilities of getting Dan to come out to help Pastor Tindall. "Let's call his father and find out where he is," Dottie suggested. "You know I think Pastor Tindall's desire to have him out here would be incentive enough." She winked at Kay.

Dottie picked up the phone and dialed Mr. Collins's number in Clayton, New Mexico. There was no answer. Turning to Kay she said, "Why don't you put in the call later in the evening. I've got to be getting home."

That evening Kay sat staring at the phone. Should she call or shouldn't she? At last, with trembling fingers she dialed Father Collins's number.

"Hello." came his voice over the wire.

"This is Kay Forrester, a friend of your son Dan," she said, trying to keep her voice from trembling. "Is Dan at home?"

"No. He is in California," Mr. Collins replied. "Wait, let me give you his telephone number."

"California!" Kay's heart sank. "So far away!" Then her heart began to beat a little faster. "Why, I wonder if he is at Pacific Union College? I wonder if Mother has ever met him? I—I—"

"Here's the number, young lady," Father Collins interrupted her thoughts. He gave Kay the telephone number of Rose Haven.

Now Kay's heart beat wildly as she dialed the operator and put in the call. A male voice that she remembered all too well answered the phone. She could hardly speak. "Dan?" she asked.

"Yes?"

"It—it's—Kay!"

"Kay? Kay who?" came the bewildered question.

"You know, it's Kay!" she repeated.

"Kay! Kay!"

It sounded like music to have him say her name. "Yes," she repeated again, "It's Kay,"

"Where are you, Kay?" he asked. "Oh, Kay, where are you?"

"I'm at Pine Forest, Dan." She paused. Was there disappointment in his voice when he said "Oh!"

Then Kay went on to tell him of the visit she and Dick and Dottie had had with Pastor Tindall. She told him how anxious the pastor was to have him help in the series of meetings. "Is there any possibility that you could come?"

There was a pause. "Oh! Kay, I couldn't right now. I just couldn't leave before September or October. You see, my Jaguar is broken down. I've had to send all the way to England for parts. It'll take two months to get the parts and get the car going."

Another pause.

"Kay! Kay! Are you still there?" Dan's voice came loud and clear.

At first Kay only nodded, her throat too choked to reply and her eyes filled with tears. Then realizing he couldn't see her, she said, "Dan, if you wait, the old adversary will see that you will never come. I must go now, good-bye."

12

The End of the Detour

Dan still held the receiver to his ear. "She's hung up! But she called!" He placed the receiver on the hook and turned from the phone with a shout. His eyes beamed. "Mother Moore! Mother Moore, do you know who that was on the telephone?" he asked.

Mother Moore stood in the doorway, smiling. "It must have been Kay. Who else!"

"She suggested I come to Tennessee and help Pastor Tindall in an evangelistic series there. He wants me. And—" he paused— "I think Kay would like me to come too."

"Well, I am sure they both would," Mother Moore looked up at Dan. "Whatever you do, let the Lord guide, Son. Remember this, we love you here at Rose Haven, and we'll miss you if you leave; but we want your happiness and the best for you."

"How can I ever order and get a cylinder head for the Jaguar in time?" he talked more to himself now than to Mother Moore who stood nearby.

"Mother Moore," he said finally, putting his arm around the

little woman who had been like a real mother to him, "Kay is worth the financial loss. I'm going to give up my Jaguar and get a cheaper car that will meet my needs. I want to see Kay and to help Pastor Tindall."

The days that followed were full of activity. There was notice to be given the hospital. He wanted to talk with each of his patient friends and encourage them. He had to sell the car and find another that would suit his needs. There were the preparations for the trip and the good-byes to the many friends he had made and the last few hours with his loved ones at Rose Haven.

But at last Dan was on his way. Beside him on top of the seat rode a small white kitten that had adopted him. Out of his rear view mirror he watched the little family at Rose Haven waving good-bye. Then he turned the corner and they were lost to view.

By the following Sabbath he would be at Pine Forest Academy. He would see Kay again, and of course Dick and Dottie, and then he'd see Pastor Tindall.

The miles rolled by. He and the little white kitten drove for long hours each day. The last few days seemed endless. It was late Friday evening when they at last reached the campus. Dan could hardly wait until Sabbath morning to walk into church and surprise Kay. Then all would be well. From little things she had written to her mother who had shared the letters with him, Dan felt that Kay still cared for him. And now he would see his beloved again.

Dan walked into the little campus church with a song in his heart. He searched the congregation for that dear familiar face. Kay was not there. Neither was Dottie, but at last he spotted Dick. Between Sabbath School and church he made his way over to Dick.

"Dan!" Dick stood up and pumped Dan's hand up and down. "Dan! I just can't say anything. It's good to see you. Sit down."

Dan accepted the invitation. "Where's Dottie?" he asked, wanting more than anything to say, "Where's my Kay?"

"The girls went with Professor Johnson to the Birmingham Church. They left quite early this morning. They were to sing a special number. They'll both be so happy to see you. Unfortunately they won't return until almost sundown. We'll wait for them at our place. You will come home with me, won't you?"

The ministers took their place on the platform and the two friends listened to the service. However, in Dan's heart was a certain urgent beating. How could he wait so long now to see the one he cared for more than anyone else on this earth.

He and Dick spent the Sabbath talking and studying together. The sun had set when the door opened and Dottie burst into the room. "We just heard at the dormitory that you were here, Dan." She gave him a big hug. "It's so good to see you!"

Dan's eyes rested on the slim figure and glowing face of the girl who had followed Dottie into the room. She was holding out her hand to him. But Dan, released from Dottie's embrace took Kay in his arms.

"It has been so long, Kay," Dan held Kay's hand as he escorted her back to her apartment that evening. "Why did you break the engagement?"

Kay stopped. "Me, break the engagement? Oh, Dan, why did you stop writing?"

Then they both learned that the months of their separation had been so wasted. "It was all a misunderstanding," Kay said at last as Dan squeezed her hand that lay in his.

"Wasted months, and yet there must have been a purpose," Dan replied, smiling down in the darkness at this wonderful girl that walked by his side. "Well, from now on we'll make our plans together," he added.

But he hadn't counted on the coolness that he found on campus among the faculty and staff. It was evident they didn't want him there. He couldn't understand why they urged him to leave Pine Forest and go to Wildwood and take up his studies there.

Before he left one evening, Dick laughingly said, "Don't you know what the trouble is here, Dan? They are afraid you've come to take their school nurse away. She means a lot to Pine Forest, and here you are and they suspect your motives."

Pastor Tindall and his wife took Dan in at Wildwood. Dan told them about his discouragement in not being able to continue at Pacific Union College.

"Well, don't be discouraged," the pastor said. "You don't have to attend college to be a literature evangelist. You have the vision. Go see the brethren, and they will put you to work."

Dan decided to return and spend the weekend at Pine Forest with Kay. It was Friday evening when he arrived. They drove out to a little church not far away for vesper service. On the way Dan told Kay about his experiences with Pastor Cox in evangelism back in New Mexico.

"Dan, that's our vision—to help others. Why don't you drive over on Sunday morning to see if you could help the brethren set up for camp meeting. I'll be out for the weekends at camp meeting. We'll see each other then."

The brethren gladly assigned work on the campgrounds to Dan. While he worked at setting up tents, he talked to them about canvassing. When the workers went to the dining hall for meals, Dan went to his station wagon. His funds had completely run out. His kitten, now a full-grown Manx cat, was still with him. Dan knew poor Tom was hungry. He felt hunger too. After the second day without food, Dan took the cat and went over to the cafeteria. The women working there seemed to take a great liking to Tom, and they offered him food. Dan then suggested that perhaps each day they would give him some food for Tom— "Not garbage," Dan said with a smile, "but the scrapings from the pans."

"Of course," the cook said. "We'll be glad to do that."

From that time on, both Tom and Dan ate in the station wagon and were happy for the food provided.

At last camp meeting started. On the Sabbath day Kay arrived. Dan noticed the happy smile on her face when they met. What a high day that was!

Tom and Dan were well fed that weekend. Kay and Dottie had brought plenty of food. The company was the best, and Dan felt sure there had never been such a wonderful Sabbath since that one back in 1962 at the Oklahoma City camp meeting, but at this one, Kay was by his side.

After camp meeting the union publishing director told Dan he could go to Birmingham, Alabama, and colporteur there.

Two hundred miles from Kay! Well, if that was the Lord's will that he work in Birmingham, he wanted to do what the Lord wanted him to do. "Don't worry, sweetheart," he said to Kay. "The conference headquarters is only fifteen miles away from

Pine Forest, and I'll need books to deliver. I'll pick up my books at the conference office, and you can be sure we'll see each other too."

"Here are three sets of *The Bible Story*, one *Bible Readings*, and three *Ways to Happiness*," the publishing director told him as he presented him with the books to sell. "This should last you for a week."

Dan had the books sold in two hours. At each home he gave a personal testimony of God's love and care for him. He always suggested a word of prayer before he left.

In the evenings, when his day's work was over, he always wrote a paragraph or two to his beloved Kay. In one of his letters he mentioned the sad time just before his first trip to Rose Haven and then the experience of being told he was not college material, but he added, "Now my heart is thrilled. Only the Lord can know how happy I am for you, when so many times I thought I had lost such a wonderful girl, then to have that closed door opened by the Lord. Making it possible for us to work, pray, and worship together is something more than I can understand. But I am so thankful for it."

Another time he wrote: "To be able to share this life with you, Kay, will mean so much to me. To be able to study together and work together in the winning of souls for Christ will be a wonderful experience of itself; but to be in the kingdom together—words cannot tell what joy that will be. When we meet loved ones, and those we have had a part in saving, that will be wonderful too!"

Dan, full of courage because of his understanding with Kay and his success in the colporteur ministry started out one morning in his car. He had asked the Lord to bless him and care for him in his work that day. Then as he drove along, the car suddenly stopped. He was twenty miles from town. Lifting the hood and tinkering around with the mechanical parts of his car he found the distributor wire broken.

Dan decided that the only thing to do was to hitch a ride to the nearest garage where he could get a part. Car after car passed him. No one stopped. Feeling a little discouraged, he looked once again at the broken wire. "Well, I know who can help me," he said aloud. He closed his eyes and sent up a silent prayer, "O

Father in heaven, I need help. I leave it all with Thee." He paused, and before he said "Amen," a car stopped beside him.

"You need some help?" the driver asked. "Look, I'll take you where you want to go. Hop in."

At the garage some miles down the road, Dan was not only able to get the distributor wire he needed, but the mechanic went back with him to the car and stayed with him until the car's motor purred and was ready to go.

"What do I owe you," Dan asked.

"Two dollars."

He looked in his billfold to pay the mechanic. He could find no money. "I'll write a check," he offered.

"No, I can't take a check," the mechanic replied.

Dan fumbled through his billfold again. Then he zipped open a section he never used. There in that section were two one dollar bills.

Dan went on his way rejoicing. God had supplied his needs. He went about telling everyone he canvassed the good news of a constantly loving and caring heavenly Father.

But Dan knew the old devil would try again and again to discourage him. His old station wagon that he had purchased in Saint Helena was fast wearing out. The water pump gave out. In trying to repair it the mechanic ran into other problems that demanded attention. And he had to wait for parts to be sent from Birmingham. The repair bill was already over forty dollars.

"Well, Lord, if You want me in this work, You'll see to it that I have transportation," he prayed.

One day he had the offer of a Volkswagen. The purchase price was low. Dan discarded the old Plymouth he had bought in California and took the VW.

"God has provided," he wrote to his Kay. "God has provided more ways than one. He has provided a wonderful Christian girl who in a few months will share my life."

13

Companion for Life

The days were full as Dan went about his literature ministry. But somehow it seemed a long time until the day rolled around when Kay and he would take their vows to love, cherish, and be true to each other throughout their lives here and to spend eternity together.

At last the day came. Early in the morning Dan went with Dick and Kay's younger brother Dale to pick up the wedding cake. "It's perfect!" Dan exclaimed when he saw it. "Everything is perfect. What a day!" Carefully the fellows placed the cake in its box on the back seat of the car. "It's a piece of art." Dan smiled as he lifted a corner of the box cover to take another look.

"Well, maybe you'd better forget the cake for a bit and think about getting ready to see your bride. Hope you'll like what you see then too," Dale clapped Dan on the shoulder.

The three got into the front seat of the car and began their drive back to the campus. "Take it easy over this stretch of road," Dan warned Dale who was driving.

"This must be like the old corduroy roads back when," Dan said, bracing himself.

When they took the cake from the car, they found that one side had been smashed. It took some doing to repair it, but when the cake had been set up, the damaged side turned toward the wall, no one would ever know.

Nothing, not even had the cake been totally damaged, could spoil this wonderful day for Dan.

It was a glorious afternoon. Dan thought that the sun had never shone so brightly and the bird's songs had never sounded so sweet. He stood at the front of the chapel waiting for his bride. The organ music flooded the room. Dan's heart pounded. There at the entrance to the little sanctuary stood the girl of his dreams, her hand resting on her brother Dick's arm.

Slowly, oh, so slowly, they came down the aisle toward him. Their eyes met.

"This is my bride," Dan thought. "She is the most beautiful girl in the world. This girl will be my helpmeet, my companion through life."

And now Dan took a few steps toward his bride. Suddenly Kay began to sing. Dan had never heard her sing so beautifully. He couldn't help the tears that filled his eyes. This girl, his bride, was singing, "Together with Jesus life's pathway we tread." And she was singing just for him. There was a slight tremble in her voice, and for a moment Dan thought she wouldn't go on, but she continued on a perfect note.

The couple walked up to the altar together and joined hands while they made their vows to each other, and Dan solemnly kissed his bride.

"Intreat me not to leave thee, or return from following after thee; for whither thou goest, I will go; and where thou lodgest, I will lodge: thy people shall be my people, and thy God my God." Dan strained to hear the words that Kay repeated before they were introduced to the friends as Mr. and Mrs. Dan Collins.

After the reception, Kay turned to her beloved. "Dan, I'd like to share a little of our happiness with my patients at the hospital who couldn't attend our wedding. Would you mind?"

"Mind, my darling!" Dan slipped his arm around Kay's waist.

"One thing that has always attracted me to you was your thought-fulness of others. Let's go." And with their arms about each other they walked over to the hospital to greet each of Kay's patients. Then they made their way to their honeymoon cabin, a little rustic log cabin beside a glassy lake in Clarks State Park, Mississippi.

"You know," Dan whispered to his bride, "I am so thankful to my heavenly Father for bringing us together in spite of all our mistakes and grief. I owe Him so much."

Kay, sitting close to her new husband, her head resting on his shoulder said, "I know. I know how you feel. Let's do something special for the Lord on our first day together."

They agreed that there was nothing they could do of greater value than visit from house to house and tell of what the Lord had done for them.

"We'll take some of our truth-filled books with us, and we'll invite our neighbors here to become acquainted with the Saviour we know and love."

They started out in the morning to share their faith. At one of the homes they found a teacher who had been holding classes in a local Catholic church. Kay and Dan showed her *The Bible Story* set.

"That set would be wonderful to have in my teaching," she said. "But right now I am so concerned about my little girl who is sick."

"What seems to be the trouble?" Kay asked.

"We don't really know," the mother answered.

"I am a nurse," Kay said. "Perhaps I could help you."

The mother led Kay into the child's bedroom. Kay put her hand on the little girl's flushed forehead.

Dan stood in the doorway and watched his Kay.

Kay asked for some ice water. When it was brought in, Kay sponged the little one's burning body. Dan sent up a silent prayer that the fever would subside. He felt sure that Kay was praying too. When at last Kay had finished with the treatment, the little girl was resting quietly, the fever had left. The child fell into a sound sleep.

"I—I—don't know how to thank you," the mother repeated over and over. "What would I have done without your help? I am so glad you came. You know, I really think I should have those books."

So the newlyweds sold a set of *The Bible Story*, they helped a child, and they had witnessed for their Master.

That evening Kay and Dan decided to take a trip across the lake in a motor boat that had been lent to them. It was on the way back that trouble began. The motor began to sputter and miss. Then it stopped completely. Dan cranked and cranked. The motor would start, however, they would go a short distance only to stop again.

"Well, I'm going to open the throttle wide this time and see what happens," Dan said, as he stood up and jerked the rope. As he did so, the boat leaped forward. Dan lost his balance, and the next thing he knew he was sputtering and flailing his arms in the cold water of the lake. "Well!" he thought, "the motor will give out before the boat goes too far." But this time the boat kept right on going.

"Dan! Oh, Dan!" he heard Kay's anguished voice as the boat sped away from him in the gathering darkness.

"Turn the motor off!" Dan, who could not swim, yelled, while trying to keep calm and tread water.

Then he saw that Kay, who had turned off the motor, had picked up the oars and was trying desperately to row the boat, but she was going in a big circle.

For a moment Dan felt panic overcome him. "Lord!" he cried, "is my life going to end this way? I'm tired. I can't keep up much longer. Please, help me."

Then he heard Kay call, "Hold on, honey, I'm coming."

He saw that she was indeed rowing the boat toward him. And as she pulled alongside, he put both arms over the side of the boat and held on until he had enough strength, with Kay's help, to clamber into the boat.

After a few more days at their honeymoon cabin, Kay and Dan returned to work, Dan colporteuring and Kay nursing at Pine Forest. A few months later the way opened for them to go out to California and work at Saint Helena Hospital. They were happy in their work, and Dan spent many hours after his regular shift studying the Bible and committing scripture after scripture to memory.

A year later the couple received a call to Eden Valley, a self-supporting institution, to serve as nurse and maintenance man. Kay and Dan accepted the call.

They had started their life together with Christ as their Companion and Example. They would go wherever He led the way. Once more Dan started for Tennessee, but not alone. His beloved companion was by his side.

"Our home," Kay said as they settled at Eden Valley, "will always be a place where angels love to dwell."

"Right, my sweet," Dan agreed, "a little taste of the heavenly Eden on this earth."

14

In the Organized Work

Dan longed to learn more about soul saving. He talked about salvation to everyone he came in contact with in his maintenance work. "Someone has to buy sheets and gowns, beans and potatoes, and all the other necessities and see that things are looked after, I know," Dan told himself. But he longed to be out doing evangelistic work. One day, unable to let things go on another minute as they were, he drove over to the conference office.

"I have a burning desire to do something for the Lord in the line of evangelism," he said. "Have you anything for me?"

"Well, Dan," the conference president said, "we think you should go back to school and take theology."

Dan remembered his experience at Pacific Union College. He remembered what Pastors Tindall and Cox had told him. If there were only something he could do within his limitations.

"If you will let me visit the families who are taking Voice of Prophecy lessons and those who are discouraged or have fallen away, I will willingly work for six months without pay," he said.

"Dan, why don't you talk to Pastor Gunnar Nelson," the conference president suggested. "He's the conference evangelist. Maybe he can suggest something."

Dan went immediately to Pastor Nelson's office. Not finding him there, he went to his home. He told Pastor Nelson his burden. Then he asked, "Could I go through a series of meetings with you just to stand by and observe?"

Pastor Nelson shook Dan's hand. "I'll be glad to have you as my assistant, Dan. I am starting a new series right away."

Dan went home whistling. He had the names of several families to visit and the assurance that he would be learning more about soul winning. He swept Kay off her feet and swung her around.

"Well, what did you expect?" Kay smiled at her tall husband. "You've always had a vision!"

The six weeks series of meetings went by swiftly. Dan's enthusiasm grew with every day. He was now doing the type of thing he had always wanted to do, encouraging and teaching others, and being a part of the organized work of the Lord.

Dan hated to have the meetings end, but at the close Pastor Nelson said, "Dan, how about joining the evangelistic team in Loveland, Colorado? I'm to start work there as soon as we wind up here."

Dan and Kay moved to Colorado. "Not more surely is the place prepared for us in the heavenly mansions than is the special place designated on earth where we are to work for God," Dan often said to his wife. "I have found a great joy in being part of the evangelistic team. I want everyone to know of the love of God and how He can reach down to the lowest man or woman and lift them up. I know, because I was one of them."

During the work in Colorado, Dan and Kay met Loretta. Loretta had attended all the meetings, and she stepped out for baptism.

"You should attend an Adventist school, Loretta," Dan remarked one evening not long after Loretta had been baptized.

"I'd like to do that," the girl said. "But where would I get the money for boarding school fees? It's out of the question."

Kay had not taken part in the conversation. But now she spoke up. "Dan, what about Mother Moore at Rose Haven? You know how much she loves helping young people. Do you suppose she could take Loretta in?"

"There's no reason why we can't find out. Mother Moore's heart always seems to have room for one more. Rose Haven would be a wonderful place for you, Loretta." Dan went to the telephone and dialed the number of Rose Haven in California.

"Mother Moore," Dan said, after greeting her and exchanging a few pleasantries, "we have a young lady here who has just been baptized. We feel she should be in one of our schools. She needs some financial help, and we were wondering if you could take her in at Rose Haven?"

There was a pause.

At last Dan hung up and turned to Loretta and Kay. "Sorry," he said, "there is just no room at Rose Haven right now."

Loretta shed a few tears. It was while Kay was trying to comfort her that the phone rang and Dan picked it up.

"Yes! Yes?" There was a pause. "That is wonderful. We've prayed about it. The Lord is so good." Another pause. "OK, we'll let you know when she will arrive in San Francisco so someone can meet her. You won't be disappointed. Good-bye."

"What was all that about?" Kay asked.

"The Lord has provided again," Dan said. "Mother Moore says that she's found a home where Loretta can stay during the week, and she can be at Rose Haven over weekends. Isn't that wonderful?"

Kay and Loretta, arms around each other, jumped up and down for joy.

"You'll not be disappointed, Pastor Dan and Kay. I can never thank you enough for taking me in and telling me about the Lord and teaching me His great love," Loretta said, her eyes shining with happiness. "You'll see, I'll go to that college in California and repay you for your kindness by helping others as you have helped me."

"That is all we ask," Kay said, going over to stand by Dan.

The months passed by quickly. Dan and Kay were planning for their first Christmas together as husband and wife. They were decorating their tiny Christmas tree when the telephone rang.

"Now who could that be," Kay said, picking up the phone.

After answering, she turned to Dan, "It's for you. The conference office is calling."

"But who is at the conference office at this hour? They were supposed to close early today." Dan took the receiver and said, "Hello!" After listening to the speaker at the other end, he said, "Of course I'll go immediately. What's the address?"

He scribbled the address on a pad by the phone, hung up, and turned to Kay, "Honey, a fellow in a bar called the conference office. He needs help. They've tried to locate a minister without avail. Now they've called me." He paused. "You know, the Lord knew a young man was going to need help, and somehow He kept that conference office open." Dan placed a kiss on Kay's forehead and left as quickly as possible.

It was already dark. The address was in a very poor area in the town. The streets were not well lighted, and Dan well knew the actions of certain gangs, how they called out to people in secluded places and then beat them and stole what they could from them. He wished he'd brought his flashlight from home. With great difficulty Dan found the house. He made his way gingerly along the side of the house to a door in a recessed area. Suddenly Dan heard a low growl. A cold chill ran up his spine. Then from seemingly nowhere a huge dog leaped up at him. Dan turned and hurried away. "What am I doing down here in this dark section of town full of gangsters and mad dogs?" the thought ran through his head and he started for his car.

But another thought came, "Are you going to let a dog keep you from winning a soul? After all, you are here now." Dan thought of times that he had been found in alley brawls. He thought of the need of the man who had called the conference office.

Dan turned and started back to the house. The dog leaped at him again and growled. But Dan, with a prayer in his heart, spoke sternly to the dog, "Down! I'm going in there, and no dog will stop me. Down! I say."

The dog growled again, but backed away, and Dan knocked loudly on the door. There was no answer. Feeling around on the door he found the bell and pressed on it. Immediately the light went on inside the house, and Dan could hear footsteps hurrying to the door.

A man opened the door and shouted, "Come in! Come in! Are you a minister?"

Dan stepped into the hallway and nodded. "Yes, I am a minister. What can I do for you?"

The man seemed quite distraught. He led Dan down a flight of steps into a basement apartment. Then he turned and caught hold of Dan's coat. "Is my probation closed?"

Dan saw the pleading look in the man's eyes.

"Tell me," he went on, "is my probation closed?"

Dan placed his hand on the man's shoulder and looked into his eyes. "Tell me, brother, why do you ask? What is your name?"

"Art Smith," the man replied. Then he told Dan about his fears and again asked, "Is my probation closed?"

Dan had never heard such pathos in a man's voice. "Art," he said, "let me ask you a question: How would you reply if Jesus Christ were to come into your apartment right now, and He would say, 'Art, I love you. I've come to wash your sins away if you will accept My love and follow Me every day'? Would you let Him come in and do as He said?"

The young man who had sat down on a chair now slid down onto his knees. "Yes, oh, yes, I'd do it. I'd do it."

Then Dan went on quietly, "Would you do it at any cost? Would you be willing to make a complete U-turn in your life? Would you be willing to give your life over completely to the power of the Holy Spirit and walk in the footsteps of Christ?"

Tears streamed down Art's cheeks. "I would. I would be willing. I would be eager. I'd say Yes to Him."

Dan knelt beside the young man. "Art, I feel confident your probation is not closed. Jesus Christ has permitted you to come to the end of your rope, so to speak, for a purpose. He wants you to accept Him tonight. Right now. He wants you to give up your way of life and make a complete surrender to Him and be willing to fight—you will have to fight spiritually, brother."

Almost in an inaudible voice Art said, "I'll do anything. Anything."

"Then let's pray right now," Dan said, putting his arm across this brother's shoulder. "Let's ask Him to fill your life with His Spirit as you dedicate yourself to Him."

At the close of the prayer, Dan said, "Art, you are smoking, aren't you?"

Art nodded Yes.

"All right, Art, bring me your cigarettes, pipes, ash trays, everything. Lay them down here on the table."

Art got up and brought his cigarettes, his matches, his pipes, his ash trays and placed them on the table."

"Have you any liquor?" Dan went on.

Again Art nodded.

"Bring it, Art, and set it down with these other things," Dan urged.

Art brought his liquor bottles and put them on the table.

"Art, is there anything more you can think of that the Lord wants you to give up?"

Art shook his head slowly. Then he stopped. He walked to the refrigerator, opened the door, and took out some bacon. From a cupboard shelf he took a container marked pepper. These he brought over and placed on the table. ·

"I—I was brought up an Adventist," he said.

"I suspected as much when you called the conference office for help," Dan said. "Now, friend, is this all? Is there anything else?" Dan motioned toward all the things on the table. "Let's pray once more and then expect victory from heaven to overcome the appetite you have for these things."

After prayer, Dan suggested that Art get him a paper sack. "I'm going to put these things in a sack and take them with me."

"Wait, there's one thing more," Art interrupted. He left the room and returned in a few moments with a revolver in his hand. "Here," he said, "I won't need this anymore."

Then Art told Dan what he had planned to do with the revolver. "I had waited so long for a minister to come that I had decided to end it all. I had given up hope. So I picked up the revolver, placed it to my temple, and was about to pull the trigger when the doorbell rang."

Dan shivered. "You mean it was that close?" He thought of the dog that had been so ferocious. He thought of his fear of that part of town. How thankful he was that he had pressed on—that his finger had found and pressed the bell at that moment! The sound of the bell had given Art hope. The Lord had not forsaken him.

For a moment neither spoke. Both men seemed conscious of God's leading and timing. Then Dan, remembering the wily ways of the evil one after he had made his commitment, said to Art, "Get your things together, brother. I'm taking you home with me. I'll spend every spare moment of my time with you studying."

"Well, that's a bargain," Art agreed and was soon ready to leave.

When they arrived at the house, Dan introduced Art to Kay. "We are so happy to have you share this Christmas season with us," Kay responded. "Come, help us finish the tree. I decided to wait until Dan returned to put the final touches on. Isn't this season of the year wonderful? It may not be Christ's actual birthday, but it does turn many people's hearts to thinking of the gift of Jesus."

"Ah, yes, you are so right," Art answered. Then he poured out his story.

"I lost my home," he said. "Just a few weeks before Dan found me I had beaten my wife so badly that she had been taken to the hospital. Then she left me, and I was unable to find her. I became so despondent that to take my life seemed the only way out. It was then in desperation I called the conference office and asked to see a minister." Art always paused at this point. A new light came into his eyes as he went on. "But God did not forsake me. He knew the exact time when I needed help most, and He sent it to me."

In the days that followed Dan and Kay watched the transformation taking place in Art's life, and Art expressed over and over his appreciation for the sweet atmosphere in this dedicated home.

One evening as Art and Dan were driving home after helping another of Dan's friends, Art said, "Say, Dan, I have a brother that doesn't live far from here. He's a big fellow, six foot six inches tall, and he weighs two hundred pounds. He was brought up an Adventist just as I was, but we turned away when we were young. I'd like you to talk to him."

"I'll be glad to," Dan answered. "It's too late this evening. We'll do it another time."

"We are so near his place, Dan. Couldn't we stop by tonight?" Art urged. "Just turn on the next street. It's half a block up the street."

Dan and Art stopped in front of the brother's house. Dan paused before getting out of the car and sent up a petition to his heavenly Father for guidance. When they entered the house, Art greeted his brother who sat in a rocking chair, a beer can in his left hand. The television set across the room blared out loud sounds of shooting and shouting.

"Bob," Art said, turning down the volume on the TV set, "I want you to meet my pastor."

"Do you mean to tell me you've converted my little brother?" Bob laughed. "I tell you, he'll never make it."

"Jesus has touched Art," Dan said in a quiet tone. "He has had a new experience."

"Naw, he'll never make it," Bob insisted.

"By God's help and grace he will," Dan responded. "I am a minister of the Seventh-day Adventist Church, and we plan to baptize Art next Sabbath."

"Baptize him?' Bob guffawed. "He can never make it. You know what kind of fellow he is? He drinks. He fights. He's been in all sorts of wrecks and drunken brawls. He's been married twice. He divorced his first wife; then he beat the second one, and she's filed for a divorce and run off to Texas. He'll never make it."

Dan noticed that Art's face had blanched. Then Art slipped onto his knees beside Bob and pled, "Bob, please, believe me, brother. I am a new person. I have allowed Jesus to come into my life. It has been three weeks since I have smoked or had a drink. With God's help I can make it." Art paused. "Won't you come and see me baptized?"

"Oh, come on, Art," Bob sneered. "You'll never be baptized. The church would fall in on us if we went there together."

Dan went over to where Bob sat and said, "Don't tell me that Art can't be baptized. Don't tell me he can't make it. Not many years ago I was rough and devil-possessed. Yes, only a few years ago Jesus came into my heart just as He has come into Art's heart. Don't tell me Art isn't good enough to be baptized."

Bob seemed to shrink down into his chair as Dan went on. "Jesus came into my heart and gave me a wonderful experience. He has done the same for your brother Art. Don't tell me what Christ can do. I know. You haven't experienced it yet, but we have." Then Dan told Bob about his conversion. He finished by saying, "You know about the Sabbath, Bob, and other Adventist truths. You know what is right."

Bob sat quietly for a few moments. Then he said slowly, "I expect I know more about this church than you do. I was raised an Adventist, at least my family was. I didn't have much to do with it, but I know all about it."

Dan placed his hands on either side of the lounge chair where Bob sat huddled. "Brother," he said, "why don't you accept Christ and become a new person and enjoy the peace and happiness of knowing Jesus as a personal friend?"

Bob jumped from the chair and pushed Dan aside. "I'm a lost man!" he said. "I'm going to be lost, and I know it."

Both Dan and Art knew that Bob had been drinking. "We might as well go," Art said. "He really isn't going to be very logical. I feel terrible. He hurt not only me but his wife by the way he talked to you."

Dan and Art left the house and went to the car. Art got in and closed the door. Dan walked around to get in on the driver's side.

Suddenly he felt a big hand on his shoulder turning him around. Bob had followed them to the car. Dan's heart pounded. This man could knock him down with little effort. But when Dan looked up into Bob's eyes, he could see that they were full of tears.

"You know, I hope my little brother makes it," Bob said huskily.

Dan placed his hand over Bob's as it rested on his shoulder. "I believe he will make it. God loves you too, Bob. He loves you as much as He does Art. He wants you to make your decision for eternal life as much as He does Art. What rejoicing in heaven there was the day Art surrendered! What rejoicing there will be if you too give your heart to the Lord! You know, friend, Jesus is coming soon. Art and I would both like to know that you are going to be among those waiting for Jesus to come and to be with us throughout the ceaseless ages of eternity."

Bob stood with his head and shoulders drooping.

Dan squeezed the man's hand and added, "Bob, why don't you give yourself to Jesus tonight? I know you have been drinking and you feel like the worst person in the world, but that's why Jesus died for you." Dan paused. "Won't you take the first step, brother, tonight?"

Dan had trouble hearing Bob's answer. "I—I—I'm—not—going —to—say—tonight." He began to weep. Great sobs shook his body. He turned and started walking toward the house.

"Let me go with you," Dan started after Bob.

"No, I want to be alone."

Dan got into the car and told Art what had taken place between Bob and him. "I am sure the Holy Spirit is working on Bob's heart," he said.

"Nothing would make me happier than to see my brother give himself to Christ as I did. Do you think he will, Dan?"

"Nothing is impossible with the Lord," Dan replied. "We are going to go back to see Bob tomorrow. Tonight we'll both spend time praying for him."

The next day they found Bob a changed man. He talked seriously with them, and he wanted to take Bible studies. "I know the message in my mind," he said, "but I want to know it in my heart."

After Bob had studied for a short time, he gave himself completely to the Lord; and when Art made his way into the water for baptism on a Sabbath morning, Bob accompanied him.

A few years later Dan had occasion to visit the little church where Bob and his family had been baptized. There he found Bob the leader of the Pathfinders. His two sons, fourteen and sixteen, were junior deacons. Bob's wife led out in the cradle-roll division of the Sabbath School. His daughter was also busy in church work.

"It never ceases to thrill my soul," Dan said later, "when I think of how the Holy Spirit works in the lives of men, women, and young people to bring them to Jesus Christ. And what a joy it is to know that in a small way you have been able to help bring a soul to the foot of the cross and then to see the radiant life that follows!"

15

God's Work Goes On

Coming into the house one day and finding Kay preparing the evening meal, Dan went over to her and put his arms around her small waist. "Kay, honey, I was with the conference brethren today. They have decided to ordain me to the gospel ministry."

Kay turned in Dan's arms and looked up into his face. "We have dedicated our lives and talents to Him, Dan. The Lord has blessed our ministry. I am so happy that the brethren feel you should be set aside for the gospel ministry by ordination." She stood on tiptoe and placed a kiss on his lips.

"I take this ordination very seriously," Dan said. "They will be setting me apart for the gospel ministry, but it will really be our lives, our home that is being set apart. I could not do it alone. You have been and are my helpmeet, and so together we'll continue to work for God in a special way."

"When will they ordain you?" Kay asked.

"At camp meeting," Dan answered. Then he added, "I hope Dad can be with us and my brother Don and—"

"Oh, yes," Kay interrupted, "your visits with Don have been few and far between for the past several years. It will mean much to both of you."

"And I hope your family can be here too. Let's get in touch with each one right away and invite them so they can make plans to be here for the happy day. There is someone else I'd like to have with us too," Dan went on. "I'd like to have Mother Moore here for the occasion. She did so much for me. She is like a real mother to me, a real mother in Israel. Then there are Marilyn and Melvin Bunch, those two who took a special interest in me and invited me to the Oklahoma camp meeting where I gave my heart to the Lord. Had it not been for their interest in me, things might not have turned out as they have." Dan gave his wife a loving squeeze as they began making plans and inviting their dear ones to be present at Dan's ordination.

And at camp-meeting time Father Collins and his new wife came from New Mexico. Don came from Oklahoma. Kay's mother and brother and sister came from California, and Dick from Tennessee. Dan felt sad when he received word that Mother Moore could not be with them nor could Marilyn and Melvin Bunch. But Dan and Kay were overjoyed to have some of their loved ones with them and receive the good wishes and prayers of those who could not be there. Then soon after ordination Dan baptized Dale, Kay's brother. That fall Dale went to Union College in Nebraska, where he started to study for the ministry.

A few days of visiting with loved ones and it was time for the families to go on their various ways. Dan, now Pastor Collins, drove out to the airport with Don and his father. Don returned to Oklahoma. Father Collins and his wife would remain with Kay and Dan a few more days.

After the plane had left with Don on board, Father Collins suggested, "Let's find a restaurant and get something to eat."

After finishing their meal, they sat talking together about God's guidance through the years. They were startled by a man running into the restaurant and calling out something in an excited tone of voice and then hurrying out.

"Well, I wonder what the trouble is," Dan said. "Must be some accident. Let's go out and see what has happened."

They made their way out of the restaurant and noticed two men with long hooked poles standing at the edge of the swimming pool nearby. Immediately Dan saw that they were trying to pull a man out of the water. Dan, without stopping to think of danger to himself, jumped into the pool, grabbed the man, and lifted him up onto the walk. The man's face was ghastly white except for his lips that had turned a purplish blue color.

"He's been down there in the water too long," someone said. "No use to try to resuscitate him. He'd be a vegetable."

But Dan thought, "This man might be unsaved. If I can save him physically, there is a chance he might be saved spiritually. I can't give up without a try to save him." Dan got down beside the prone figure and began to give him mouth-to-mouth resuscitation. It seemed like hours that Dan worked. Then the man's fingernails began to turn pink. He gasped, and Dan felt a pulse beat. When the rescue squad came, the men quickly got the man into the ambulance.

Dan and his father went to the hospital. There they found a distraught wife. "Oh, why didn't they keep up with the artificial respiration in the ambulance? His heart stopped beating again." She wrung her hands. A physician standing nearby began immediately to work on the man. Soon his heart began to beat again, and his color returned.

Dan spent much time that evening praying for the man who had almost drowned. Before retiring he called the hospital. There had been no improvement. He continued to pray. When he called in the morning, he was informed that the patient was doing quite well and was mentally alert.

Kay and Dan visited him in the hospital. They gave the man the book *Steps to Christ,* and Kay sang a hymn before they left.

"Please do come again," the man said, with tears in his eyes.

"Kay, that man has been restored physically," Dan said one day after their newfound friend had been released, "but he needs spiritual healing. I pray that the Lord will show me the right time and place and give me the words to say that will be what he needs."

"The Lord has a thousand ways," Kay said as she smiled up at her husband. "Yes, a thousand ways."

And not long afterward, they were invited to have dinner with the man who had almost drowned, his wife and their friends, and a Baptist minister and his wife at the restaurant where the accident had happened. The Baptist minister had been the chaplain at the hospital when the man had been admitted.

Somehow Dan felt impressed to mention to the man how the Lord had spared his life. "If it had not been for the help you received," Dan said, "would you have been ready to meet your Lord?"

For a moment the man didn't speak. Then he looked up at Dan. "No, I would not have been ready." His hand shook as he put a cigarette to his lips while his other hand toyed with a full cocktail glass on the table.

"My friend," Dan said without a smile, "you had better enjoy that drink. It's the last one you are going to enjoy."

The man looked startled.

Dan went on. "Do you think the Lord spared your life for you to continue drinking and smoking?" Dan paused.

There was complete silence around the table. Then, laying down his cigarettes and pushing away the cocktail, the man said, "I'll never touch them again. May this be the beginning of a new life for my wife and me. Collins, I can't thank you enough for caring."

Dan looked around the table. The eyes of each was full of tears. Dan knew they were not tears of sadness, but tears of joy.

Very soon after this experience Dan received an invitation to hold the Week of Prayer at Sandia View Academy in Corrales, New Mexico. What memories rushed to mind as he drove onto the familiar campus. Scene after scene of past years rushed before him. He remembered why he had made the decision years ago to attend an Adventist school which he despised. He remembered his choice of associates and how careless he had been. He recalled how careless, yes, unruly, he had been, and all the trouble he had caused. He recalled the day the dean had told him he was being expelled. He remembered his trip home and then of his mother—of her broken heart and death. He'd let down all barriers after that. The horrendous experiences that followed made him recoil. It had all been a nightmare, but the Spirit of God had not left him. And at last he had resigned all—given himself over to one who could keep him from falling. Now here he was back at a starting place.

No one at the school knew of his past life there. That was a closed chapter. He had prepared a series of talks that he felt would help these students in their Christian work. But that first evening as he stood in the pulpit and began to speak he noticed the restlessness of the audience. He sent up a silent prayer for guidance. As he paused to send up the prayer, a quietness came over the student body. Dan then left the pulpit and took a few steps forward, closer to the students.

"Dear students," he began, looking over the now waiting group. "I know that some of you don't want to hear the message I have prepared for you this evening. I have decided not to preach to you now, tomorrow evening, or the next day." He paused again.

All eyes were on him as he began to tell the students the story of his life. He told them of his restlessness, his indifference, his turning his back on God, but all the way through the story there was the working of the Holy Spirit—that drawing power that would not forsake him. One could not help but feel God's presence in that chapel.

When he sat down, the students made no move. They seemed not to be conscious of the passing of time. At last, very quietly and slowly they left the chapel.

It took much out of Dan that week to tell the story of his past life, but it ended with the triumphant victory of his full surrender and his determination to let God lead him. " 'Not more surely is the place prepared for us in the heavenly mansions than is the special place designated on earth where we are to work for God,' " Pastor Collins said. "My friends, God is so good. He can take your life as He has taken mine and can make something worthwhile, useful, and beautiful out of it. 'There is no limit to the usefulness of one who, by putting self aside, makes room for the working of the Holy Spirit.' You will never know the joy of living until you have tried letting Jesus come into your heart." He ended the Week of Prayer with an invitation to each one to try Christ and His way of life.

Dan's heart was full of joy as he left the campus after seeing a great revival take place. How different from the time he had left years before! How he wished Kay could have been with him. She would have been such a wonderful help in visiting, encouraging, and counseling with the students. But Kay had not been able to go. Now Dan looked forward eagerly to going home.

Dan and Kay had received a number of calls from various conferences to join up with them as an evangelistic team. Somehow they felt impressed to wait. Then one day they received a call from J. V. Stevens, president of the Arizona Conference. "Dan," Pastor Stevens asked, "have you made a commitment to accept a call yet?"

"No, we are praying about it, asking the Lord to lead us where He wants us," Dan replied.

"I'd like to talk to you about some plans in the Arizona Conference, Dan. I'll be in Denver next week. I'll see you then."

Dan and Pastor Stevens met and spent days together talking about the Lord's work. Dan listened while the conference president told about his burden for Arizona. "You know, Dan, three of our men have recently lost their lives in an airplane crash. We'll probably not know in this life why such a thing happened, but God's arm is not shortened. I was supposed to be with those men," his voice shook as he went on. "I couldn't go because of a previous engagement. Since my life was spared, I feel more determined than ever to speed the message of Christ's coming."

Then he went on, "Dan, we'd like to have you in the Lay Activities and Sabbath School Departments of the conference. You'd be working with laymen and in soul-winning activities, teaching how to give Bible studies and follow-up work. Now, brother, talk it over with your wife and pray about it.

Dan and Kay talked and prayed about the call to Arizona. They felt impressed that they should go there. Dan called Pastor Stevens and told him of their decision. Then they flew down to Phoenix to look for a place to live. Having been in the Air Force, Dan was eligible for a G.I. loan, and they found the home they wanted just four miles from the hospital in Tempe where Kay would be nursing. It was only a short distance from where the new conference office would be. Back again in Denver, they began sorting and packing their things. At last the day came when all their stuff was packed and ready to be loaded onto a truck to be transported to Phoenix. But before the truck came, Dan received a phone call asking him to attend a meeting in Cheyenne, Wyoming. The North American presidents and the publishing leaders were to meet there. They wanted Dan to be present.

"Now, why do you suppose they want me at such a meeting?" Dan turned to Kay. "This is going to mean a delay in our move to Phoenix. I'm to travel to Cheyenne with my old friend Gunnar Nelson. He's accepted a call to the Washington Conference," Dan said.

"Well, I'm sure the Lord will lead us," Kay answered.

"Thanks, my dear, you are always ready with just the right words of encouragement." Dan smiled at Kay.

En route to Cheyenne, Dan listened to his friend Pastor Nelson talk about evangelism and the needs of the Washington Conference for men fully dedicated to the Lord's service. Dan was at a loss to understand why at this time he was hearing so much about evangelism. When he arrived at the meeting in Cheyenne, the brethren there talked to him at great length about going into evangelism. "Dan, you are cut out for evangelism. We think it would be a mistake for you to take on another type of work. If a call came to you from the Washington Conference for evangelism, would you accept it?"

Dan felt perplexed. "I owe an obligation to the Arizona Conference," he said, "but, brethren, I do believe in counsel. If the General Conference leaders through the Pacific Union and the Arizona Conference see the Lord working in this and decide that I should go to Washington, I will accept. But there must be no injured feelings."

Once more back at home in Denver he told Kay what had happened.

"Well, I want the Lord to have His way in our lives. We'll just pray and wait," Kay said.

"Right," Dan agreed.

"I'm sure the Lord will make His will plain if we wait upon Him." Kay smiled up at her husband.

Telephone calls came from the General Conference, from the

Pacific Union Conference, and from the Washington Conference. At last Dan received a phone call from J. V. Stevens in Arizona. "Dan, we release you from your call to Arizona. Whatever the Lord has in mind for you, do it with all your might, and God bless you."

Dan was now ready to go to Washington. The truck came and was loaded, and headed north instead of south. But there was the house that they had arranged to purchase in Arizona. What about it?

"Will we be able to recover the money we put down on the house in Arizona?" Kay asked.

"That we'll have to leave up to the Lord," Dan told her. "Come on, sweetheart, we'll begin house hunting in Seattle immediately when we arrive."

The first day they saw so many homes that Kay dropped wearily into a chair when they returned to the Nelson home where they were staying for a few days. She rubbed her aching feet. "Dan, we've seen at least thirty houses today. Not one seems suitable. If they are suitable they're out of our price range."

"I know." Dan stood looking out the window. "I know, but you've said it many times, 'Our heavenly Father has a thousand ways—' Let's pray about it."

About five o'clock the telephone rang, and Mrs. Nelson called, "Dan, an agent is on the phone for you."

Dan hurried down the steps and took the receiver. "Hello!" he said.

"Mr. Collins, I think I have a real tip. A friend of mine just called about a house that I think is just what you want. Can we run out and look at it now?"

"Of course. Thanks very much. We'll be right over," Dan answered. He hung up and went up the stairs three at a time to tell Kay the news.

When they reached the house in a newly built up section of town, Kay's face lighted up. "Oh, Dan, it's just what we want. Isn't it beautiful?"

"It sure is. But it's probably out of our price range."

"Let's go in," Kay urged.

When the agent came and Dan asked the price, Kay gripped

Dan's arm. She had to ask the agent to repeat the price. She looked at Dan, and Dan looked at her. Their eyes lighted up.

"God answered our prayers," Kay said softly.

"If things can be worked out with the agent in Phoenix, we'll take the house," Dan said.

"Well, I'll do my best," the agent reached out to shake Dan's hand. "I'll get in touch as soon as possible. Now how late can I call you?"

"You call any time the agreement is worked out," Dan said.

At 1:00 a.m. Dan and Kay received word that the house was theirs. By 1:00 p.m. the next day their furniture had been moved into the place and things set in order.

"How good is the Lord!" Kay said as she snuggled against her loved one as they had their evening worship in their new home. "If only everyone would trust and pray and wait. The Lord is willing and eager to work out all one's problems."

"Yes, and the Lord knows that we have only a short time before our first evangelistic service is scheduled and there is much to do. He didn't want us encumbered with house hunting at such a time." Dan grinned down at his wife by his side.

"The Lord has so many surprises for us, and He supplies all our needs according to His riches in glory," she said softly.

"Let's not become too attached to this place." Dan smoothed Kay's silky hair. "You know, we will not be able to be in our home when we are carrying on an evangelistic campaign. We'd better find a trailer that we can use for such purposes. We can move it from place to place—a home away from home." He laughed. "It won't matter to me so long as you're there."

The trailer they needed was found and purchased, and then Dan went to talk to the conference brethren about help.

"We'll supply you with a minister of music," the conference president said.

"Well, my wife is well qualified for that job, and I would like to work with her," Dan replied.

"Fine! Fine!" the president agreed. "Since she is a nurse, she can help you with the health phase of the work too."

"You know, Kay," Dan said to his wife after returning from his visit to the conference office. "I've asked to have you as my assistant. You'll look after the music, won't you? And I'd like to have you give a fifteen minute health talk each night. And, did you know that when I was a boy I lived in Bremerton where we'll first open? It was during the second world war. Dad worked in the shipyards there."

Dan and Kay worked hard in Bremerton. The meetings were well attended, and it was a happy couple that prepared forty people for baptism as a result of the evangelistic meetings combined with the working of the Holy Spirit.

Moving from place to place, holding one series of meetings after another, struggling with people's problems and pleading with them to surrender themselves to Christ was not an easy task for the young couple; but, as Dan said, "The Lord has done so much for us, how can we do any less for Him?"

They were to hold a series of meetings in one of the churches in the conference. The time for the opening meeting came. The church was nearly full. Dan and Kay were in the ministers' room praying and waiting for the time for Kay to go out and start the song service. From time to time Dan looked out through the slightly ajar door to see the people taking their place.

His face shone as he turned to Kay. "The Lord has really blessed tonight. What a congregation! It's time Kay!" Dan reached out for Kay's hand, and once more they prayed for God's help and guidance.

Kay stepped out of the ministers' room. Dan watched her as she took the three steps up to the platform where she would cross the baptistery and then step onto the rostrum. Then he saw her hesitate, stumble, and fall.

Suddenly Dan realized that the old baptistery cover had been left off. His Kay had tripped and had fallen into the baptistery. In a moment Dan was bending over her, "Honey, are you hurt? Do you think you can stand?"

Kay grimaced. "Oh, Dan! The pain! I—I can't move my foot."

Dan lifted her up in his arms and carried her to a chair. "Sit here while I get a doctor." He saw the grimace of pain on Kay's face. "I'll be right back," he promised.

Dan hurried to the phone and called the doctor who lived just a few doors from the church. Then he hurried back to Kay. "The doctor'll be here in a few minutes, sweetheart. I guess you won't be able to be on your feet for a while."

"Dan, I've been praying about this. I am sure I can stand up." With that she rose to her feet and walked without effort to the rostrum and started the song service.

When the doctor came, Dan pointed to where Kay stood on the platform leading out in the song service. "There she is, doctor. It's a miracle!"

The doctor shook his head. "Yes, if she took the tumble you say she took and she was in such pain she couldn't move her foot, it is a miracle. Well, another Physician got here first, that's all I can say." The doctor slapped Dan on the back.

Dan preached that evening with such fervency that the audience seemed spellbound. The following night the crowd was larger than ever.

A few nights later the weather turned cold, and a heavy snowfall made travel difficult. "I wonder what this storm will do for our meeting?" Dan said to Kay on the way to the meeting place.

"Well, we can be sure the old devil will be happy if the attendance falls off. I have a feeling he thought my fall and hurting my ankle would be a stumbling block. I'm so thankful that the God whom we serve is able to keep us and His power is greater than the evil one."

Two night's later Dan awakened in the night. He groaned as he turned over. Every bone in his body seemed to be aching.

"What's the matter, darling?" Kay asked, touching Dan. "Why, you're burning up with fever! I'm going to take your temperature." She got out of bed and went to get the thermometer.

"I feel terrible!" Dan groaned before she slipped the thermometer under his tongue.

All the next day Kay kept Dan in bed and brought him fruit juices to drink and sponged him to get the fever down.

"I've got to get up and go to the meetings," Dan insisted.

"But—But—you can't—"

"Weren't you the one that said the other night the devil was trying to stop the meetings? Is this the way he is going to succeed? No, Kay, God will give me strength to do His work."

Dan did not miss a meeting. But he could not visit the interested ones during the day. How could he bring them the message when he felt so weak?

There were times when he had to hold onto the desk to keep from falling while he was preaching. At times the words blurred as he tried to read texts from the Bible; but Dan had all the texts memorized so that he did not have to read them.

The crowds kept coming, night after night. Dan had just enough strength to carry him through each meeting; then Kay would drive him home and put him to bed. Each day she prepared the sermon in her mind in case she would have to take Dan's place. But night after night, although the faces in the audience blurred before him and he had to hold onto the desk and the words of the sermon blurred, he carried on.

"It's 'not by might, nor by power, but by my spirit, saith the Lord.' " Dan muttered as he fell exhausted into bed one night.

"You've got to see a doctor," Kay insisted.

And at last Dan agreed.

"I can hardly believe how you have carried on the meetings with your physical strength being so drained!" the doctor exclaimed. "Do you realize you've had pneumonia?"

16

A Sermon to Be Remembered

Far out in California, Mother Moore and her family at Rose Haven had thought many times of Dan Collins, the young man who had come to their home several years before, discouraged and broke. Mother Moore remembered the Dan who had returned later to go to school at Pacific Union College, so full of hope and expectations of taking the theology course and going into the ministry. She had so many times spent the evenings talking to him and encouraging him and praying with and for him. He was like one of her very own sons. She felt a great burden for this young man. She had felt so many of his joys and sorrows. She thought of the happiness it had been to her and her family to know he was taking for his wife Kay Forrester, a Christian nurse.

How eagerly Mother Moore had looked forward to letters from them and how proud and happy she was for his success now that he was in the organized work! She had wanted so much to be at his ordination, but that had not been possible. But now her Dan and Kay were a successful evangelistic team. They were soon

finishing up a series of meetings in Port Angeles, Washington. That was only a couple hundred miles from where her daughter Marcia and family lived, and she was going to visit Marcia! Right then Mother Moore determined that this was her chance to see Dan and Kay too.

Soon after arriving at her daughter's home in Camas, she asked them if they knew that Dan and Kay were in Port Angeles holding an effort.

"Why, Mother, no, we didn't know. Phone them, and we'll drive over this weekend," Marcia insisted.

It took very little urging for Mother Moore to call Dan's number. How her heart beat when she heard his deep voice say, "Hello, Pastor Collins speaking."

"Dan?" Mother Moore said.

There was a pause.

"Mother! Mother Moore!" Dan's voice came over the wire. "Where are you?"

"I'm with Marcia here in Camas, Dan. If it's all right with you and Kay, Marcia and Norman and little Randy will bring me over next weekend. I do want to see you both so much."

"All right? It's perfect. We'll be so glad to see you all. And, Mother Moore, I am holding my last baptism here next Sabbath. It will be so wonderful to have you here for that. You are somewhat responsible, you know."

Mother Moore couldn't help the tears of joy that came into her eyes as Dan told her about the baptism and that she in a way had been responsible for the occasion. What a thrill to see this young man, her Dan, and his wife Kay again and to know that she had had a little to do with influencing him for the right.

It was late Friday afternoon when they arrived at the trailer home of Dan and Kay. Kay greeted them with open arms. "Dan isn't home right now. He's out visiting and counseling with those he feels need a little more instruction before their baptism tomorrow. Oh, come in! Come in. We've been looking forward so to this visit." Kay, her arm around Mother Moore, led them into the comfortable home.

There were so many things to talk about. But Mother Moore

kept listening and waiting for Dan to return. The hours passed. The clock on the mantle chimed 1:00 o'clock before Dan walked in, a happy, expectant smile on his face as he gathered Mother Moore into his strong arms.

After a short but refreshing sleep Mother Moore with Norman, Marcia, and Randy drove to the church with Dan and Kay. Mother Moore enjoyed Sabbath School, but this morning she could hardly wait for the service to begin.

There he stood at last on the platform! A tall, broad-shouldered man of God.

How his mother would have thrilled to see this son, the boy who had given her so much sorrow and heartache, the boy who had constantly turned away from her in his teen-age years! Now here he was dedicated to the task of bringing others to Christ. Mother Moore's thoughts raced on.

She thought of the times he had felt the wooing of the Holy Spirit and of his attempt to do right and how he had stumbled into the snares of the evil one. And then at last, the miracle! She was startled from her reverie as she heard Dan's voice:

"Dear brothers and sisters, this is a great day for me." There was a pause. Pastor Dan Collins looked over his congregation. "This day I share your joy in knowing that you have accepted Jesus Christ as your personal Saviour and are signifying to others this commitment by being baptized today. My joy is compounded by the knowledge that God has used me in a humble way to bring this message to you.

"Many of you have had real problems to face. Many of you are still facing problems." The pastor paused again. Then, leaning over the podium he spoke to a family in the front row, calling the man by name, "Rodney, isn't the love of God wonderful? You took your stand just last Sabbath, and that presented a problem."

The man nodded.

Pastor Collins now spoke to the congregation. "Rodney's employer insisted that he work on God's holy time. When he could not change Rodney's mind, he suggested he drive the truck only part of the day. But Rodney stood firm. Praise the Lord, friends, that the Lord gave him victory to stand firm and true. Praise the Lord for Robin, his helpmeet, who encouraged him and stood

by his side helping him to stand for the right."

There were "Amens" heard throughout the church.

"I had planned to tell you the story of my conversion; how I finally came to know and understand my Saviour's love. You have heard me refer to it time and time again. How a young couple who were farmers came into the store where I worked. It was after I had begged God to leave me alone. They came into the store and through their warmth and love invited me to have supper with them. Then they invited me to a religious meeting—a camp meeting. I tried to run away from God. I didn't want to stay for the meeting, but their kindness won me over. I stayed. That night I saw the love of God and His mercy as I had never seen or heard it before. I saw the plan of salvation. This poor wretched sinner took his stand for Christ. Brothers and sisters, it was no less than a miracle.

"I have someone here this morning that I take great pleasure in introducing to you. She is a mother in Israel if there ever was one. She has many extra sons and daughters, and I happen to be one of her extra sons. And I want you to know that she loves me as much as any mother could love." Pastor Collins's face shone.

"Mother Moore, will you please stand up? Marcia and Norman and Randy, will you stand with her?"

Mother Moore got to her feet.

"When she met me," Pastor Collins continued, his hand outstretched to the little white-haired woman standing with happy tears in her eyes, "I was in a bad way, but God sent me to the right place, at the right time—and to the right mother. This is the mother of the farmer's wife in Woodward, Oklahoma, where I had been working in a store. What a blessing this family has been to me.

"Here in this church we are a close family. This is God's family. God opens doors, and the doors He opens are safe to step through. My prayer for each one of you is that you will always be a part of God's family, holding open the doors He opens for you and gathering others into that fold within the family of God."

Pastor Collins spoke to the little flock as a family. He called the family members by name and commented on their faithfulness and his great joy in seeing them share their faith. He spoke

to the children and to the youth. "I know, Susann," he said to
one young lady that appeared very timid, "that it took a lot of
courage to walk up to your employer and say, 'I am going to be a
Seventh-day Adventist.' What an experience we have had in this
church! I hope it will never be the same again.

"That brings me to the center of my message this morning—the
task of the church. My burden is not only for those who have
been in the church a number of years, but for you who are new in
the faith. You have all studied and are moving in the right direction. God has plans for your lives."

A silence had settled over the congregation. Mother Moore
turned slightly to see how these dear people were responding to
the message. The congregation seemed to be leaning forward,
breathless, their eyes fixed on their pastor, drinking in every
word he spoke.

Pastor Collins went on to speak about the relationship and
responsibility of each who has taken Jesus to dwell in the heart
and home. He spoke about God's love for the sinner but His hate
for sin. "Sometimes," he said, "we become a little confused in our
thinking, we don't have to love the things that are so repulsive
to love the person.

"According to Romans 3:10, 'There is none righteous, no, not
one.' Verse 23 says, 'All have sinned, and come short of the glory
of God.' And this morning we need the cleansing blood of our
Lord Jesus Christ. This gift is so precious and is freely given to
each one of us."

Time slipped by. No one seemed aware of the passing of time as
the pastor talked on, encouraging, exhorting and commending
the flock.

Then, later, in robes of azure blue they walked down one by one
into the baptismal font and were buried in baptism. How their
faces shone with joy as they walked up the steps in newness of
life. Seventeen persons that day, making thirty-nine members
in all, were added to the little church at Port Angeles as a result
of the efforts of the team of workers with Dan Collins who had
dedicated his life to God's work.

"It is true," Mother Moore said to Kay at the close of the service; "there is no limit to the usefulness of one who who laying self

aside makes room for the working of the Holy Spirit."

As good-byes were said and Mother Moore was ready to return to Camas with her daughter Marcia and son-in-law and their child, she exclaimed, "Oh, the majesty of it all when the clouds will be rolled back and the starry heavens shall be seen in all their beauty and Jesus will come. What an occasion that will be!"

She turned to Dan. "Oh, Danny," she said, looking up into his face, "what an occasion when your guardian angel presents you that morning to your dear mother! I can just hear her shout, 'Danny Boy, praise God; you're here!' "

And now there were tears in the eyes of the tall pastor as he looked down into the eyes of this little mother who meant so much to him and who had taken the place of the mother who had been laid to rest. There were tears in his eyes, but his face was wreathed in a smile as he said tenderly, "Yes, I remember she told me I was a special child sent from God. It took many years for me to understand this. But on that resurrection morning Kay and I are determined to be there to welcome her and all those loved ones that will be raised to life immortal. And we'll all go into the kingdom together and give praise and honor and glory forever to the One who has led us all the way."

Mother Moore got into the car. She waved to Dan and Kay until they could no longer be seen standing by their trailer home. In her heart she knew that Dan and Kay would not be standing alone on that resurrection morning. There would be a host for whom they had all labored and prayed.

She folded her hands in her lap and bowed her head.

"Dear Lord, please save the children Thou gavest me—
Those bound by chords of suffering and prayer—
And Father, remember each adopted one;
They, too, must meet me there. Amen."